Life in Art and Practice

Stories from my Younger Self

Other work by Mari Howard:

NOVELS:

Baby, Baby (Science, faith, and prejudice)

The Labyrinth Year (Art, science, & losing your way)

ORIGINAL POETRY:

Live, Lose, Learn: a poetry book

learn more at:
hodgepublishing.co.uk

MARI HOWARD

Life in Art and Practice

Stories from my Younger Self

HODGE PUBLISHING

Published by Hodge Publishing
10 Bainton Road, Oxford, OX2 7AF

ISBN 978-1-7398710-0-0

British Library Cataloguing in Publication Data

A catalogue for this book is available
from the British Library

Cover design and typesetting
Rachel Lawston, Lawston design

CONTENTS

AN AUTHOR'S NOTE

These short stories, written between 1989-2003, come from a world which was not only pre-pandemic and pre-Brexit but pre-mobile phones and largely pre-internet usage and social media. Before 9/11, and everything that led to it. A big worry was, of course, HIV/AIDs, but for many in the West, life was good, it seemed a 'stable' world, a place of flourishing. 1989, the Berlin Wall was torn down... what could go wrong?

But what was that past, the place we look back to, really like?

While writing these, I was studying for a Certificate in Social and Political science. I had 3 school-age children at home, worked for a short while as an occupational therapy assistant in the local hospital's geriatric medicine department, and was specialising a bit in health care. I'm also a painter. My inspiration continues to lie in the dynamics of human relationships, and the wider society's influence on our lives. The stories combine magical realism with social issues, touching on ambition, fear, mental health, hope, despair, teenagers, and the longings of our hearts.

Appletime

(1996)

The ant was struggling uphill over the worm cast. It was impeded in its progress by the size of the breadcrumb it was carrying. Abby Evesham, lying on the picnic rug under the pear tree, turned away, put out her hand, and lazily stroked Tabitha, her cat. The cat's fur was fiery hot from the sun which sloped between the branches of the trees, blazing out of a pure sapphire sky. Abby sank her fingers into Tabitha's thick, butterfly-marked fur, feeling the softness, the warmth, the luxury of it, until the baby in her womb kicked her under the ribs, giving her a start. Quickly she moved her hand to feel his limbs where they seemed just under her skin — the scan had shown she was expecting a boy, and his vigorous movements made her sure he would be, like his father, energetic and athletic, an outdoor kind of person.

Maternity leave was almost upon her: thirteen weeks officially, elongated if she could find a locum willing to stay and able to work well with the other partners — Richard, her husband, with whom she job-shared, Lucien the new boy at the practice, and Joshua, known as Josh, the senior partner. Abby closed her eyes and lay on her back: the sun shone red through the lids, and the weight of the baby on her internal organs soon made her turn over to a more comfortable position on to her side.

She dozed and woke, lay in the shade of the tree watching Tabitha chasing a bee around the nasturtiums. Twisted noses — that was what nasturtiums were, old-fashioned flowers which had grown in her grandmother's garden, orange and yellow and pungent-smelling, with hideous, creepy blackfly lurking silently on the backs of their funny circular leaves. She had hated and feared the blackfly, lurking like a disease, hidden corruption. Plant diseases were like that: distorting the leaves, twisting the stems, canker and leaf miner, mite and rust. She had wanted her grandmother's garden to be perfect — she had wanted the world perfect, and it was the insult that disease made to the world which had made her want to train to be a doctor, to fight disease and corruption.

It was late August, and the apples and pears were forming on the trees, burgeoning along with her baby. They had moved into this house a year before, anticipating a family. She loved the house, a cottage with a small garden which had once been part of an orchard. She loved job-sharing — such a sensible, go-ahead idea, they had wondered why more of their friends didn't do it. The patients were quite happy once they understood that half the week Dr Evesham meant Dr Richard Evesham, and the other half Dr Abigail Evesham: once her pregnancy began to show, some of them had made approving remarks about how sharing jobs and sharing parenting would help the Eveshams give their best to both their patients and their family. Joshua had been fine about it: Joshua was a wonderful, positive person. Abby shut her eyes and thought of the perfect baby forming within her:

she knew he was perfect, she had had all the tests. A perfect baby, a perfect house, a perfect family… Dreaming again, she was shocked into wakefulness by the image of something disgusting — she didn't know what — moving across her path, casting a shadow as it moved.

'God — Lucien!' She opened her eyes and there he was, standing over her, dangling his stethoscope from one hand.

'I'm sorry — did I give you a fright?' he grinned: perfect teeth, if large.

She laughed, leaning on one elbow, pushing back her long black hair with the other hand. 'What are you doing here? Why are you waving that thing around?'

'Waving it? I was just folding it up to stick it in my bag. Dashed out of the surgery with it in my pocket - you know how one does. I had this brilliant idea I wanted to run by you and Richard - do you have a moment?' Lucien squatted beside her on the humpy, worn-out summer grass, and clicked open his bag to stow the stethoscope away. Inside, for a moment Abby expected to see - what? Phials of glittering colours, spices with strange scents? She saw only Lucien's prescription pad, his torch in its black case, little envelopes of antibiotic starters, ampoules of opiates and a packet of tongue suppressors. His shadow fell across the rug, and over her body, cutting off the heat of the sun.

'Tell me?' She said, struggling to her feet and brushing crumbs from her late lunch - a Danish pastry - off her cut-off maternity overalls. She shoved her feet into her sandals. 'Richard's out for supper - got a meeting - I can supply you with cold beer and quiche if you haven't got something better at home.'

'Wonderful.' Lucien smiled his wide smile, stood up and

removed his jacket. 'I envy you two. You're so domestic.'

Abby caught sight of Lucien's car, a black sports saloon Toyota, parked on the gravel path at an angle. Like Lucien had dashed up the drive and screeched to an emergency halt. 'I envy you your car!' she said.

'We could go for a drive,' Lucien said, 'goes like a breeze. Wonderful engine. Purrs like a tiger.'

'I think I'd rather have the quiche,' Abby said firmly, as she felt the baby kick again, 'and hear about your idea.'

She took the supper out onto the patio, under the wisteria. 'No beer for you?' Lucien asked.

'Strictly no-alcohol pregnancy,' Abby said, and she giggled. 'Gosh, I sound so pi.' She sipped orange juice, and broke off a forkful of quiche. 'This is something I'd only do for a baby. Spill the beans, then.'

'Well – fundholding, in a word, is on the way out. I was thinking of going entirely private – GPs' practices are small businesses, and with medical insurance spreading among the population, we could do a lot worse than charge for our services. I think we'd see an improvement right across the board.' Lucien sipped his beer, looking at her with narrowed grey eyes. He winked. 'Abby – do you want a car like mine? Private schools for your kids, no more disturbed nights?'

She shook her head. 'Becoming a doctor, my father said, meant becoming everybody's servant. On call twenty-four hours a day. That's how Dad was. We never knew, if we sat down for a meal with him, whether he'd be called out. And of course, that meant he didn't read bedtime stories, things like that.'

'Hence job-sharing?'

'Yes, if you like. I worked my butt off to impress Daddy

– get equal, do something he'd respect. You know he didn't come to my graduation? Too busy delivering someone's kid.'

'You resent his involvement, yet you followed him into the profession.'

'I said: I wanted to get equal. I wanted to show him I could do it. And – and this is important – I want to show my kids it can be done without sacrificing them.'

'Basically, wouldn't you say the patients exploit us?' Lucien said, and he put his head on one side.

'You mean, out of hours? Phoning when an aspirin is all that's needed? Calpol, and reassurance? I don't know – if you thought your kid had meningitis, wouldn't you call an expert?'

'I think — and I feel a lot of people agree – that they're a generation who've grown up with a free service, and they just regard the doctor as a mug you can call on when you've forgotten to buy indigestion pills. Time was when every parent knew Granny's recipe for croup – now I have to go round and advise on boiling kettles to make steam, and goodness knows what else – give sick notes for Monday morning on Sunday nights… They just think because we're free we're there to serve…'

Abby found Lucien's words discomforting, but weren't they true? Didn't he have a point, and a valid one? She laid her hand on her full belly, and reassured herself of the comfortable bulge that was her baby. 'A private practice? Tell me more – would that get rid of on-call?' She asked.

'I can see it – a clinic where we ask patients to come to us, evening surgeries after working hours for commuters – then total shutdown all night, with perhaps a triage team of nurses manning — womaning that is – phone lines. Yes!' Lucien stood and punched the air. 'Great idea, Lucien! Say it - old Josh is going to have to comply with the majority, and BUPA or some such organisation will fund the appointments, not the nanny state. Now the restrictions of the Red Book are off, the sky's the limit! '

He sat down again. Abby thought a few minutes. 'What about the old people who can't pay?' She asked. 'What about the families up on the estate? There are single mums who haven't got transport…'

'And how did they get themselves into that mess?' Lucien asked. 'Are you saying we have a duty to get them out of it? Come on, Abby - you're a doctor, not a social worker!' He picked up an apple from the plate of fruit Abby had placed between them, for dessert, and began to peel it, round and round, making a perfect long snake of the skin. She watched a moment, thinking about what he'd said.

'I don't know. It makes me feel uncomfortable, somehow.'

'Abby, darling Abby — you realise GPs are technically private consultants. You always knew that. It's just a little adjustment. Don't worry about the patient's private circumstances — you aren't responsible… Think of your family — you do want Richard to be able to read those bedtime stories and play with them in the bath, don't you? You don't want to be a deserted wife, a practice widow?

She shook her head, picturing Richard with their perfect child. 'You're persuading me, Lucien,' she said.

'Wonderful.' Lucien held out the apple. 'Marvellously juicy. Have a bite?'

*

Later, under the apple trees in the moonlight, Abby and Richard walked hand in hand. The dogs gambolled and sniffed around their feet. Suddenly, the cat, Tabitha, sprang from the shadows, and rushed wildly up the trunk of one of the trees, making the branches shake and the apples dance and judder. An apple fell, plop, at Abby's feet. She picked it up, rubbed it on her overalls, and put it to her mouth, biting into the sweet, firm flesh. She saw Lucien in her mind, and remembered his proposal.

'Darling, Richard, listen. Lucien's pretty bright, isn't he?'

'He came with excellent references. Josh was impressed.'

'He's a good doctor, isn't he?'

'He's fitting in and developing nicely, the patients like him, yes.'

'He was round here today. Talking about practice developments.'

'And what are these, that I haven't heard about? There isn't another practice meeting till next month. Lucien hasn't become privy to something Josh's been doing that we haven't been told about, has he?'

'Don't worry. He's told us his plan before mentioning it to Josh. He said a bit about the idea of exploring going totally private. He said there's a whole range of things that could open up now the Red Book's restrictions have gone.'

'Well, well, well.' Richard shook his head. 'A high flyer. He'd better look out if he isn't going to crash.'

'Darling — I thought that. But now I'm not so sure. Minor surgery clinics? Our own lab — our own hours — the hours we choose — sold to the patients as more convenient for commuters, of course. All out-of-hours at our own emergency clinic, no nasty visiting people's dreary homes in the middle of the night, and independence from the Health Authority. We'd be in direct competition with the NHS — that can't be bad, we could create the opportunities we think are most needed, in the way we see them, without being answerable to anyone but ourselves.'

'You're convincing me,' Richard said.

Abby held out the apple. 'One of our first. Very sweet and crunchy. Take a bite, darling?'

*

Traces of the overnight frost still lingered on the roof of the health centre as Abby arrived for morning surgery. It was one of those iron-grey days in the depths of winter: the sky a steely mid-grey, the cold intense. Inside, Lucien would be closeted in his office with their accountant, studying the books. Abby sighed, as she picked her way carefully between the two rows of rose trees which bounded the path up to the Garden Health Centre. She was wearing a pair of crocodile-look high heels today, and frost-covered, slithery leaves from the apple and pear trees growing on the lawn in front of the building lay everywhere.

The new health centre was built on their old orchard garden. Colin, and Adrian their younger child, had had to make do with a much smaller garden, but the nanny used to take them to the park to play, and later their main hobbies were computer games and competing at the local virtual reality centre. Even so, Colin, as a small child, kept a little garden where he learnt to plant seeds and watch them grow; while Adrian had always loved animals, so much so that, even as late as his eighteenth birthday, he had had a tank of lizards in his bedroom, and a rat in a cage.

Abby pushed open the door. She walked through to the reception area, blinking in the fluorescent lights after the dim grey light of outdoors. Outside, it was as if the sun had fallen from the sky, but indoors was warm, bright, electrically intense, the air trembling with anticipation of the patients — their source of revenue. Behind a computer, the head receptionist was typing in details of the morning's lists, while in the background two others of the office staff were busy answering phones.

The atmosphere in the waiting area was of cushioned warmth — a rose-pink carpet, rose-pink covered upholstered chairs, and pink paint combined to suffuse the room with a warm glow. A bowl of pot-pourri stood on the coffee table, surrounded by the latest editions of Vogue and Country Life magazines, and editions of the quality daily newspapers.

'Your first appointment's at eight-forty, Dr Evesham,' the receptionist said, rubbing her hands together, indicating the cold of the weather outside. 'Cold, isn't it? I've upped the heating.'

'Thank you, Janet. I'll be in my room if anyone wants me.'

Abby fished the keys out of her handbag, and unlocked the door of her consulting room. For a moment it appeared in the dimness of the early morning, as a dark grey cave: the instruments lurking on the trolley, the couch a slab, awaiting a body. The weight of darkness pressed down on her head. Then she flicked the light switch, and a beautiful room appeared. Painted golden-yellow, with flounced curtains and a comfortable couch surrounded by all the latest equipment, including a small ultrasound scanner for gynaecological exams. Abby specialized in women's health problems — so many women preferred another woman to give them intimate examinations, she'd found, and the NHS obs and gynae specialists were nearly all men. How could men understand the vicissitudes of the curse? What did they know of the pain of childbirth?

She took off her coat, and hung it up, sat down at her desk, and kicked off her shoes. Off-guard a moment, the emotional despair of the past few months flooded her brain, and she let it circulate, from her brain to her limbs, until she felt the tingling all over. Adrian was dead. At eighteen, with all his life before him. And Colin had been arrested and charged. Colin, her perfect first-born. Later today, she and Richard were due at the inquest.

She thought of buzzing Richard, who would by now have arrived in his consulting room across the corridor. No. Richard must mourn in his own way — Richard was angry, angry about the pile of work running a private practice had turned out to be, angry that Lucien absented himself so much, often to closet himself with the accountant. Counting the takings, Richard called it. She suspected what Richard got up to when he didn't come home till well after nine some evenings. He said it was the pressure of work – the commuters' clinics, anything. He said what a sweat it was, being at everyone's beck and call, slogging his guts out day after day.

She suspected he was seeing his first wife, Lily. Lily had haunted her dreams when she was pregnant, especially the second time. She dreamed that Lily would turn up at the hospital and snatch the baby away – for Lily herself was barren, she'd had PID when she was 17, and IVF hadn't worked for her. That had led to Richard and Lily's divorce.

The thought of Lily swirled around her brain. Lily had got wind of their plans to go private and tried to interfere. Neither of them had listened, of course.

God. She'd like to have talked to Josh – he had always seemed so wise. She reached out for her bag, opened it and took out her stethoscope and torch, laid them on the desk, switched on the lamp. Then she took out a syringe and an ampoule of diamorphine. To soothe her emotions, she told herself. Abby rolled up her sleeve, found a suitable vein and injected into it.

On top of all this, Colin's girlfriend, Josh's daughter Marianna, was due to give birth. Marianna had got pregnant without Colin knowing, while he thought she was on the pill. Colin had claimed it must be Adrian's child. The marriage had all been arranged – white wedding, honeymoon in the West Indies, the lot. A tear dripped onto her desk.

Then the drug hit like two strong gins, straight to the bloodstream, and Abby felt the immediate relief. Why was life such a bummer, that she needed heroin to feel human?

*

'Abby, love, a word.'

Lucien was standing out in the cold, clutching his trench coat around his still lithe body. He was a sportsman and it showed: middle-age wasn't a problem. The winter dark wrapped the health centre round like an icy cloak, and the cold was, again, intense. Visibility was impaired by a damp mist, clinging and miasmic. Abby's legs, in sheer nylon tights, were covered in goose bumps, and her short skirt didn't help. She shivered, thinking of the warmth inside her car, once she had scraped off the ice and got the heater going.

'Abby! Don't run off, lovey!'

She turned. It had been a long, hard day at work, after the inquest. She wasn't keen to hang around chatting to Lucien. She wanted to get supper on – indeed she was even wondering if she could persuade Richard to take her out to supper. 'Yes?'

He seized her by her coat collar, and looked deeply into her eyes. 'Look, the fact is, we're in debt.'

'Okay – I thought we always were – I thought the accountant ran the overdraft, and the bank were understanding about the new equipment. After all, my scanner's going to create much more work – new patients, new money.' She smiled. 'Lucien, let go of my coat. Richard will suspect us.'

'I hardly think so. This is urgent.'

'So is getting home. Can't this wait till the practice meeting? We're in debt – what's new?'

'I thought you could break the news to Richard. It's serious debt… The accountants are really bothered.'

Abby's stomach lurched. Before she could think of anything to say, Lucien switched his tone. 'Any news about your grandchild, lovey?'

'No news yet. We'll be going up to the hospital as soon as there is any, of course. But we don't know it is ours – it could be anyone's. It's Josh's grandchild, that's certain.'

'She's so young – too young. Typical of today's youth, don't you think?'

'Whose side are you on, Lucien? Let go of my coat!'

'I always wanted you, Abby. I've been jealous of Richard all these years.' His hair was still blonde, streaked with grey, his skin was hardly ageing. How did Lucien remain so young?

'I'm sorry. And now – well, I'm almost a granny, as you so carefully reminded me, after all!' She forced a laugh, and he suddenly let go of her coat. 'I'm going home, Lucien, and I'll hear all about our financial troubles at the meeting.'

Despite this Abby felt a deep, agonising worry about what Lucien had said. Being responsible for their own finances, being totally independent, wasn't easy. It was, they'd found, a hard furrow to plough. She and Richard had often spoken of how much easier it must be for Josh, still part of the health service. And she felt guilty that what she offered wasn't available to everyone, regardless of ability to pay.

She started her car, and drove out into the traffic. It was eight o'clock, and the crowds had thinned, until she came into the shopping centre and found cars jammed nose to tail along the main street, their brake lights glowing red in the fog, a debased form of Christmas decorations. Overhead, the city council's offering – giant stars and fir trees picked out in electric bulbs – spanned the street. Christmas shoppers crowded the pavements. There were people disembarking from minibuses and picking their way among the cars.

Was it one of those special shopping nights the Round Table organised just before Christmas?

She sighed and in despair put on the handbrake and the radio. O Little Town of Bethlehem was playing on classic FM, and the trees in Debenhams' windows were winking their lights. Suddenly the carol stopped, and the radio announcer said, 'Dr Evesham? Is Dr Abby Evesham out there?'

'Yes, I'm here,' Abby said stupidly to the radio, then realised of course it couldn't hear her. 'Does somebody want me?'

'Marianna's baby is born — this is a message for Dr Abby Evesham — go to the hospital immediately!'

Joy to the World played as Abby disengaged herself from the traffic jam in the main street, and drove off up a side road far too fast. Her grandchild! It might be — she wanted it to be...

Floodlights beamed over the hospital, but despite these, a great star was visible in the deep navy winter sky. Abby parked in the staff car park, recalling that she had often legally parked there, when she was working in the GP Unit delivery suite. She ran towards the lift, and squeezed in just as the doors began to close. It was crowded with new fathers, clutching carrier bags of clean nightwear, bunches of flowers, and baskets of out-of-season fruit. She was conscious that she was grinning with excitement, as she glanced round at the other passengers. On the fourth floor, she stepped out into the fluorescent light of the maternity ward.

As she approached, the nurse at the desk said brightly, 'Marianna Davidson? Oh yes — the single mum in room nine.'

Abby noticed that Marianna hadn't checked in under the name of Evesham — perhaps she hadn't wanted the hospital staff to know the connection with the Evesham practice. Instead, she'd used her father's surname. Her father, Dr Davidson. A single-handed doctor. A doctor who ran a practice in the poorest part of town.

Room nine was clean but oddly shabby, with an iron bedstead and faded striped curtains, not one of the private rooms. Inside, Marianna sat up in bed, cradling her child. Around the bed were gathered a bunch of rough sleepers and one or two of the Down's Syndrome people Abby had noticed getting out of their bus. She had the strangest sensation that although the rest of the hospital was lit by fluorescent lights, room nine was darkened, lit only by a gentle suffused light above the bed. The effect was similar to something she had seen on Christmas cards.

Abby dropped onto her knees, and bowed her head, catching sight of the card on the baby's cot. A blue card, giving the name Joshua Davidson. The picture in her mind blotted out the scene in the hospital a second: Lucien tumbling from a great height into a well of darkness, and at the same time, the child with his arms stretched out, perhaps to embrace her.

She turned, hearing a noise outside the room. The senior obstetric consultant and the chief executive of the hospital trust were talking in low voices in the corridor. 'Quite irregular, completely unthinkable,' the consultant was saying.

'But think — born to be king. The astrologers were absolutely certain.'

Abby was never certain afterwards whether she had heard this or not.

Willow

(C. 1989)

We were in the pub down by the river, Nick and I, sitting at one of those round corner tables for two. The table was ringed with the marks of beer glasses, in spite of the mats advertising lager, but the place was a good-quality bar. There were stuffed fish in glass cases on the walls — a good big spotted trout eyed us from a case — and little coloured flies in cases decorated the mantelpiece, above the fire with ornamental plastic coals.

Nick drank lager: I drank gin and tonic. I remember I was wearing my khaki combat overalls that evening, and silver earrings. I was psyching myself up, missing Ali and feeling cold.

'Another drink?' Nick asked, scraping back his chair.

'Yes, please.' I pushed my glass across the table towards him. He picked up the glasses and made his way to the bar. The place was filling up with yuppies in striped shirts, open at the neck, and their girlfriends in short straight black skirts and silk blouses. Nick is the County Archivist and a conventional dresser: he was wearing cord jeans and an Aran sweater. He has little gold-framed glasses of the sort

John Lennon used to wear: I used to like John Lennon, years ago, before Ali.

While Nick was at the bar, I noticed his bottom. Some people say women like a neat bottom and slim hips on a guy: I don't know what I like, but Nick's bottom seemed to stare at me from the bar. The lines of the seams of his jeans outlined it, and I thought about touching it. Cord-covered, it was all right, but nude, skin to skin? I made my eyes travel up his back and to his hair — he's just beginning to lose his hair, but it's mousey and straight and undistinguished like Nick's whole appearance. Not that he's undistinguished: he got a First in Greats and wrote a thesis on something totally obscure, while I was scrubbing floors, and nannying, earning money to put my street theatre on the road.

The good thing about Nick — the best thing — is that we've known each other for such a long time. Twenty years, nearly.

'One gin and tonic. I bought some peanuts as well.' He put my drink in front of me. 'Okay?'

'Okay. Let's talk about something else.'

'Something else? You've been quiet all evening.'

'Sorry.'

'Are you regretting this?'

'No. I was thinking about my father.'

'Your father's a shadowy figure to me — I can't imagine him.'

'I didn't cry when he died,' I said, fumbling in my canvas shoulder bag for a cigarette. I found the packet and realised I didn't have any matches. 'He dropped dead of a heart attack, pruning his roses, and I didn't cry. Damn, I haven't got a lighter or matches — you haven't, have you? No, you wouldn't, you don't.'

I went to the bar for matches. When I came back, Nick said he could do with one tonight, even though he'd given up, so I passed the Marlboro packet across the table, and our hands touched as he took one out. Mine was cold and his was warm. I thought our hearts were like that too — he's got a wife, Jenny, and twins, and they live in a stone cottage with a dog and three cats. He'd told Jenny he was out late looking at a parcel of letters an old colonel had found in his loft. I'd said that sounded like something out of Agatha Christie or someone.

'Tell me about your father,' Nick said later back in my living room. We were on the old couch — it's hideous, a grey and red design from the Sixties, and he had his arm round me and we were drinking coffee and listening to my old *Hair* record. 'This is the dawning of the Age of Aquarius,' I sang quietly, putting my head against Nick's shoulder and longing to get myself in the mood. All I could feel was Aran sweater and my own heart jumping around, and I wasn't sure if he knew I was a virgin or not, which worried me.

'Tell me about your father.'

'He was a solicitor. Pin-striped suit and well-polished shoes. He used to ride a bicycle into town carrying his jacket in the basket. It was the sixties but he was ecology-minded — actually, he was mean. He grew roses — all through the summer he never went to work without a rose in his buttonhole.'

'Sounds a little eccentric, like you,' Nick said. He took a swill of the brandy we'd bought earlier to help us along, and then he stroked my breast, upwards, feeling for the nipple. I hadn't worn a bra in years. Instinctively, I recoiled from his stroking hand and concentrated on the vision of my father.

'He favoured my brother — you know, I think that's why I had all my hair cut off, to look like Johnny. Ronnie and Johnnie he used to call us. When I was little, he liked me best. I remember him building sandcastles with us on the beach — he always helped me more. Then I got lumpy and dumpy like Mother and he used to move away when I came into the room.'

'I wish you'd grow your hair again. I liked it long, when we were at Oxford.'

I saw in my mind Dad and Mother visiting me at St Anne's. We'd got hold of a punt and took them down the river through the University Parks, under the willow trees. Johnny was there, and he was reading Milton's *L'Allegro* and *Il Penseroso* aloud in the boat, and Nick was punting, and Mother was ogling Nick and asking if he was my boyfriend, and Dad and Johnny sat side by side in the stern, flopped back on old magenta-coloured cushions. I was wearing a flowered nightdress as a dress, and Granny boots with laces, and a straw hat.

Mother had called me my whole name — Veronica — and told me to get my hair cut and wear proper clothes. Even then, you could tell she didn't want me to run a theatre company: she wanted me to make a good marriage and turn her into a grandmother. She was knitting that day, or crocheting, I forget which, for my cousin's baby.

Anyway, the record was playing *Let the Sun Shine In* and Nick was draining his brandy. He said if we didn't now we never would, so we went in the bedroom and took off our clothes. I think he was trying to be nice, because he undid all the buttons of my combat suit and when he got it open he kissed me between my breasts. He couldn't know how I felt about that – how it made me miss Ali and shiver inside. He'd taken off the sweater earlier and so I undid his shirt and underneath he was two-coloured: tanned on the arms where he had been working in the garden and white-chested. He and Jenny hadn't yet been on holiday that year. They were going to Turkey later, he told me. Just the two of them, leaving the boys with Jenny's parents and doing a tour of the archaeological sites. Then, I supposed, he'd get properly browned.

He took off the gold-rimmed glasses which made me think of John Lennon and laid them, closed, on my bedside table, on top of *Twelfth Night*, which I'd been reading to adapt for our company to perform in the market square on August Bank Holiday. And because I didn't make a move to undo his jeans, he did it all himself, which perhaps didn't turn him on as he would have liked. He shook them out and folded them and put them on the floor.

And so to bed. Nick did all the things he said Jenny liked, and I watched him through half-closed eyes, wanting to join in and not knowing how, my body stiff and unresponsive, till I thought of Ali.

'Things getting better?' Nick asked.

'Yes, just keep doing that.' I saw my father pruning his roses, and dropping down dead among the Peace and the others I didn't know the names of, the white ones my mother called virginal. I was a virgin – should I tell Nick – would it hurt – oh God, it hurt, it hurt he wasn't my good old friend of twenty years, the County Archivist, any more. He was Man, panting over me, panting and plunging and gasping for air. Gasping 'Ronnie, oh Ronnie, love me, love damn you!'

And my body wasn't my own: it was part of Nick's. I gasped and shivered and my legs were shaking, parts I didn't know I had responded without being told.

I was ashamed at my response: I had enjoyed having Nick. We were both sticky with semen and I'd betrayed Ali.

He put on his glasses again — he can't see without them — and he was wearing nothing but his spectacles and asking me what I was thinking about.

'Your sperm wriggling up my uterus,' I said to put him off and remind me what we'd done it for. 'How about you?'

'Jenny,' he said, and burst into great sobs. Despite politics, I found it made me despise him for unmanliness: I didn't know what I was, fish or fowl. I just wished I'd been born a man.

*

Willow was born nine months later. Willow is a child of Aquarius. He lies on the bed naked and pees a great arc of urine in the air sometimes, and I laugh.

It wasn't an easy birth. I took classes in natural childbirth and imagined myself lying in a birthing pool with soft music and only the midwife, and Ali of course. I didn't want men there. But Willow was a great nine-pound lump of male flesh with a head like a cannonball, stuck the wrong way round, claustrophobic in the birth canal, and they sent a tribe of men to get him out. One stuck an epidural in my back and another pushed the bed into the forceps delivery room where the blue bright lights flared on the ceiling, and a third brandished the forceps, great bent fish slices Ali said they looked like, going up my vagina. I'd thought Nick's prick wouldn't fit, the night we conceived the baby, and now here was this great head, and the enormous forceps — birth is a terrible violence. And Willow was hauled out, screaming the place down, and thank God the paediatrician was a woman, so he was passed from the midwife to her to Ali to me, four peaceful women.

He's in his buggy now, playing eating his toes. He's a good baby, and he doesn't look like Nick at all — only a tiny bit. I'd thought of Ali's beautiful graceful dancer's body, curving in the great pas de deux I'd seen her dance over and over, and our own pas de deux, tumbling in the bed together, all the time Nick was inside me. That was what made Willow. I named him for the trees that grow by the canal at the bottom of our garden. He was born at midnight, under the moon. He's got two mothers, Ali and me. Sometimes he comes in our bed with us. my hope for him is that he'll be strong and peaceful. I put an announcement in the paper when he was born: to Ronnie and Ali, a male child, Willow. With thanks to Nick for all he's done for us.

One day, they'll let us use the sperm bank.

An Outside Chance

(1990)

The girl was just 20 — not much older than his daughter would have been. She had been married and had a year-old son, but the partner they needed to find wasn't her husband. She lived in bed and breakfast accommodation, polite language for a slummy hostel near the station.

David shook his head, thinking that in medicine one couldn't make distinctions, everyone was prey to illness, which is no respecter of persons. He had referred her to the clinic for sexually transmitted diseases, who would do the appropriate tests. What he couldn't fathom was what her parents would say—she wasn't a street kid, her father was one of the top consultants at the hospital. He shook his head again. Of course, he wouldn't tell them. She had cried and said please don't, but medical ethics wouldn't have allowed him to anyway.

She was the last patient. He stood up and gathered the papers on his desk, tidying the envelopes of patients' notes into the tray for filing. Then he opened the top drawer of the desk, took out his keys and locked it up. He did all this automatically, the picture in his brain more real than the room around him. He was thinking of Amy. Today would've been her birthday.

He didn't hear the knock or the opening door.

'I'll put the answer machine on then, Dr Mason. Any more letters?' the head receptionist asked, as she leaned into his room a moment later, still grasping the door handle.

Letters? Oh, letters, David thought. Of course, she was new since Amy happened. That was years ago. One couldn't expect her to know. The senior partner knew. All the other doctors – all four of them – were new in David's eyes.

'No letters,' he said.

'Good night, then, Dr Mason.'

He picked up his stethoscope and shut it in his bag. He went out to the car park and opened his car, got into the driving seat and thought of Tricia. This morning Tricia had shown no sign of remembering: they had talked about the cat. Cleo. She had brought them another offering, a slightly burnt pork chop. He couldn't say to Tricia, what about Amy's 18th birthday – why couldn't he say it? She had squatted on the floor by Cleo's bowl, pulling off little pieces of meat, and he couldn't talk about Amy's birthday.

Giles and Harry would be home when he got in. Thank God for Giles and Harry, normal and healthy. Tricia got pregnant again quickly, and had Giles. Harry two years later. They held their breath, metaphorically, all through those pregnancies. These days they'd have had genetic tests. Or would they? He didn't know what Tricia would've wanted.

He still felt he didn't know what Tricia wanted. He started the engine and drove home.

She wasn't there. Getting out of the car, he'd pictured her in the kitchen, preparing supper. He'd thought it would at least be a surprise for her that he was home for the evening meal, that the practice meeting he told her would make him late had been rescheduled, and they could have supper as a family. But she wasn't in the kitchen, or in the garden where he went hunting for her, imagining her picking the deadheads off the roses or finding a lettuce for the salad.

Loud music came from above. He tuned and bellowed, 'Giles! Turn down that damned racket!'

The cat came slinking from under the buddleia bush, which was covered with purple flower heads, fragrant like honey, and wove herself around his legs. She yowled, looking at him with round yellow eyes full of hunger.

'Where is Tricia, beastie?' He asked her, leaning down and stroking the brown velvety fur behind her ears. She rubbed against him, slinky and sexy, like Tricia years ago. Like Amy might have been, so svelte and elegant, if it hadn't been for the extra chromosome. What sort of a father would he have been to a girl — he hoped he'd have been a better father than the eminent consultant whose daughter he'd seen today.

Disturbed, he bellowed again at Giles's window. The music suddenly ceased.

*

He made a large Spanish omelette and a salad, telling Harry tales of his single days while he cooked. They ate it on the patio. The air was fragrant with the scent of syringa and next door's honeysuckle. A small plane droned overhead.

'You have to come to the school play, dad.'

'What day of the week is it?'

'Friday and Saturday – you must be able to manage Saturday. Don't say you're bloody well on call that weekend.'

David ignored the language, on which he had given up, and consulted his diary. 'Looks okay to me,' he said. Where was Tricia? This would be a perfect evening, but it niggled him – where was she? She hadn't been home all day. Had she remembered Amy after all? Why hadn't she waited for him?

From indoors, the phone shrieked. Giles sprang up. 'If you're not on call, that's probably Charlie.' He beat David to the hall and seized the receiver.

'When? How badly hurt is she? Where did it happen? Dad...' Giles said, holding out the receiver.

'Tricia?' David said, 'Where? No, I'll come at once of course.' He listened to the voice of the Accident and Emergency receptionist. Tricia had had a car accident. His chest seemed to cave in, he couldn't breathe, his legs were like water. He sat down, heavily, on a chair and put back the receiver. No, she wasn't dead – that ironic trick hadn't been played. Just hurt and in hospital. Her car smashed up on a country road. Where the heck had she been going?

He didn't know how to feel. Angry with her for driving without care? Or for taking off to wherever it was? Relieved she was alive. Hurt that she should hurt him on this day of all days. What would they have been doing if it hadn't been for the extra chromosome? It might have been their daughter's eighteenth birthday party.

'What are you going to do – up to the hospital straight away?'

'Yes. You and Harry stay here – you've got prep – I don't need you – she won't be able to see you. God, what a day.'

He meant, what a day to choose. He couldn't say that.

Of course, she hadn't chosen.

Or had she?

He was afraid he didn't know Tricia. The cat leapt past him, up the stairs, yowling. Why did she keep appearing as if she was Tricia's spirit? Then he realised he hadn't fed her. That was why she was following him around.

*

He realized Tricia would need some basic things. He blundered upstairs, confused with relief and anxiety, found Tricia's weekend case and shoved into it one of her nightdresses, her slippers and dressing gown, a sponge bag with her toothbrush, and toothpaste. She never squeezed the tube from the bottom – she squeezed it in the middle, she always had. He remembered packing her case for her when she went in to have Harry. Harry was early, and the contractions were coming so close together she was afraid David would have to deliver the baby himself. Sneakily, he had wished that too, but he had got her to the hospital and everything had gone as planned. He knew Tricia didn't trust him – she trusted that consultant, young Gwyn Evans.

Now he was packing for her again. After her car accident. Beside the bed lay her library book – *Moontiger* – he put that in on top of the clothes and shut the case. Passing the dressing-table he noticed her hairbrush, opened the case and dropped it in. His hands were shaking.

In the car, he turned the key and the radio came on. Radio Three, Beethoven's Ninth. In a flash, he saw the concert after he and Tricia got engaged. The *Ode to Joy*. The year he began clinical medicine, and his father had advised a long engagement. He had worked hard and they'd rarely seen each other – got married once he qualified, moved around doing house jobs, then Amy had arrived…

Afterwards he couldn't remember driving to the hospital, parking the car, going up in the lift, hurrying into the ward. He looked around the curtain, to see her, Tricia, lying in bed, her right arm tightly bandaged to her body. She looked grey and exhausted, propped against the pillows wearing a hospital nightgown. An orange plastic bowl with no fruit in it, and a plastic water jug, stood on the locker beside her. Alongside was her wicker basket, containing her sketch pad and a bunch of withered greenery.

'David. I'm sorry. I wrecked the car.'

'Don't bother about the car – how are you?'

'You can see. The van sort of got up on the bonnet and the side of the window caved in – it got my head, I don't know how many stitches. I was out a couple of minutes, more perhaps. That's why they've kept me in – they told you didn't they.'

'Yes. How's the arm feel?'

'Aching. They didn't think it was broken but they did another x-ray, and it is – just below the elbow. I won't be able to do anything useful for ages.'

'Don't worry. I'm thankful it wasn't worse.'

'It could have been. I simply didn't look, I turned this corner and suddenly – I don't know where it came from, the red van. David, I don't remember what happened!'

He took her left hand. That was the uninjured arm. 'Often people don't remember the moment of the impact. It doesn't matter.'

'What about the police?'

'Think about them when you've rested. What were you doing?'

'Driving back from my class.'

He knew she had lied. They had told him where the accident happened, the other side of town from the technical college, on the way out towards Snowdonia.

He'd suspected she had a lover for some time. He wondered how her lover would feel, seeing her now. Her face was bruised and cut, and the long dressing over the deepest, longest cut, above her forehead, was surrounded by hair matted with blood. Some of her hair had been shaved so that they could treat the cut. But her swollen eyes suggested she had been crying – maybe he was wrong, maybe she had remembered their little girl.

He pictured another time, Tricia exhausted in a hospital bed, and himself looking around the curtain. He hadn't been able to be there for the birth of his first child. He had sensed immediately something was wrong. Tricia turned her face away from him, into the pillow. Beside the other mothers, he had seen Perspex courts, each containing a tiny bundle. Beside Tricia there wasn't a cot.

'Where is she?'

'In the nursery – in the sick baby unit. David – she's got problems with breathing and swallowing and she's never going to be all right — I'm sorry, David, she's a — she's got Down's syndrome. I thought it only happened to older mothers.'

Now, eighteen years later, penitent for his suspicions, he approached the delicate and most intimate subjects which lay between them.

'Darling, did you remember today?'

'To fetch your suit? It's in the car – or somewhere they've put all my things. I don't know where.' She let go of his hand, so that hers lay limp and damp in his grasp.

'The radio was playing Beethoven – the *Ode to Joy* – just now. I had it on in the car – I thought of our engagement.'

'Maybe we shouldn't have got married.'

'Why not?'

'I only cause you problems.'

'Like this? It could happen to anyone.'

'No – It couldn't. It was my fault. I was thinking of something else, driving like a maniac.'

'Amy?' He asked.

'Sam – Sam Newell, the art teacher. I got what I deserved – he's going away, I'm never going to see him again.'

So, she had been with her lover, she had forgotten Amy's birthday. He was silent. Impotent rage tore at his guts.

'She only lived five weeks but I remember her,' he said, 'I wouldn't have abandoned her if she'd grown up. They can be very loving, Down's children.'

'You wouldn't have had to look after her. You're never there. So I found Sam… Don't stay, David. It's all a mess.'

Sam. Samuel. He tried to picture Sam. Middle-aged like himself? 'So who is this Sam?'

'I told you. Sam, the art teacher. He's getting over a disastrous marriage. He was married to Gwyn Evans's daughter – of course, she was too young, married at eighteen – what an irony, Gwyn Evans who looked after me for Giles and Harry.'

'*Gwyn Evans's daughter?*' David said, forgetting medical ethics for a second.

'Yes. Why?'

'Nothing,' he said, remembering the General Medical Council again. 'Just an irony.'

My God, the girl in the surgery. *Her* husband. Has she had sex with him recently? Who was having sex with who? Has she left him permanently for her new partner or played around? The sweat poured down the back of his neck. He pictured the forms for the test at the clinic for Sexually Transmitted Diseases. HIV? Traces of virus or no traces? When would he hear?

What should he say to Tricia?

Over the antiseptic smell of hospital, he smelt the heavy seductive fragrance of the honeysuckle, withered in the basket but still scented. He remembered Cleo, climbing in it, scrabbling up the fence, pursued by her lover, the silver tabby tom. He saw Giles and Harry. What did he say to them?

Nothing, he thought. Nothing till the girl's tests are done.

Leaving Home

(1992)

Fenny picked up her bag and threw it across her shoulder, marching away from the school gates like a yomping soldier. The bag was a rucksack, but Fenny had looped one strap across her left shoulder. With her right hand she reached into her jeans pocket to see what change she had: she was always hungry, sometimes desperately so. Her stomach would cramp, during lessons, with an agony of emptiness. Her mother said it was her age, and asked if it happened especially when she had her period? It had happened to Fenny's mother, apparently, at those times. Fenny was sixteen and a half. She found 50p, and decided to buy some chocolate.

The sky hung very low and black: maybe it would rain. Fenny waited at the bus stop, chewing on a Mars bar. When the bus came, she suddenly remembered she was adult fare now. She thought of pretending that she wasn't, but although she was thin and willowy she was quite tall and her breasts showed under her baggy cotton T-shirt where her long cardigan swung open. She wouldn't pass. She paid adult fare and found a seat. The bus swayed and bumped along the bus lane. Presently the rain began, spears of water against the windows. Her palms were damp and cold. She thought of the name of the clinic, *family planning*, and didn't know whether she had made the right decision. Looking around the people on the bus: old people, mothers with small kids, huge shopping bags, and clumsy folding baby buggies, teenagers like herself, she felt small and alone. Ultimately you were on your own: none of these people knew her or cared about her. Crowded together in the bus, each one was an isolated entity. Even if their bodies touched — and she had just shifted on her seat to allow an old man, who stank of tobacco and sweat, to ease himself down beside her — their real selves might as well not exist. They were just bodies, fleshy machines.

You were okay, if you lived only in your body and didn't let your emotions get involved. You could have a lot of fun that way, her friend Margi had said.

*

The Volvo was becalmed in a sea of traffic. Cars stretched ahead to the temporary traffic signal. Lorna stared, mesmerised, through the misty windscreen at the red tail lights of the vehicle in front. Presently they inched forwards a few yards. Lorna released the clutch. The wheels turned. The car moved forward. Then they all stopped again. She checked her watch: Amelia's cello lesson was due to start in ten minutes. There was no way that they would be across town by then.

'Ouch!' Amelia shrieked from the back seat. 'Can't you stop him? He's attacking me with his lunchbox.'

'I'm not. I was drawing on the window and I couldn't help it, could I, if you sit so near to my bag. You're taking up two seats.'

'I have to hold this carefully. It's my Elizabethan diorama. Miss Jenner said I could take it home to show Dad.'

'He won't be interested in it. He's only interested in what we do in science and games. I got in the Colts team – he's going to come and watch me play.'

'I can't believe they took you, you're such a pain. You're mental.'

'That's an insult — you can apologise or I'll smash your face in.'

'Listen who's talking – where did you learn that big word?' Amelia said. She moved the diorama carefully to her other side, in case Patrick tried any face-smashing. 'Mummy, can you put this beside the cello in the front seat,' she asked leaning around the headrest to speak to Lorna. Lorna had a cloth in her hand and was cleaning the windscreen from the inside, while outside the wipers thwacked and whacked back and forth.

'Matron,' Patrick said. 'If we talk like that, at our school, matron whips out her pistol from her knickers and you're dead meat.'

'Oh yes – prep school is for creeps and snobs,' Amelia said, ducking so that when Patrick hit her his fist passed her by and knocked against the window.

At the same time, the light changed and the traffic cleared. Lorna, taken by surprise, started the car with a sudden, jolting leap forward. She was sweating, her shirt stuck to her back under her mohair designer jumper. Her feet, in boots, felt swollen and inept on the pedals. During the jam, the car had felt like a terrible steel trap in which she was condemned to live for eternity with her two fighting offspring.

'Mum, you're making me feel sick before my lesson,' yelped Amelia.

Relieved to be moving at last, Lorna passed a tin of boiled sweets back to Amelia with her left hand, while she held the wheel with her right and followed the road around a curve. One good thought popped into her mind. No kids to shout at, no homework to supervise. Never again.

She addressed Patrick and Amelia. 'I've got my women's group this evening, so when we get back, Fenny will be in charge. Daddy will be in around seven. Be good for him,' she said. The thought of the women's group gave her a warm feeling inside, the courage to carry on.

'I hate Fenny,' Patrick said. 'She's bossy.'

*

Hugh glanced at the clock on the wall. Five o'clock. He slotted the drill back into its place.

'Sucker tube,' he said to the dental nurse. She handed over the tube. Hugh leaned over the patient, expertly catching little bits of the old filling from under the tongue. The last time he'd do this ever. It gave him a strange feeling. The last patient. She was young and South Asian. Her mother-in-law and husband were there as chaperone and translator. Her treatment was free, her belly bulged, beneath her traditional garments, with her seventh child.

'Amalgam,' Hugh said, handing the sucker tube back to the nurse.

As he filled the tooth, he took just the same amount of care as he had always done. He worked quickly, smoothing down the surface and asking her to bite and re-bite on the place, working repeatedly on shaping the filling until he was satisfied the patient was comfortable with it. He was never happy with a less than perfect job.

Finished, he sat back in his chair, tore off his protective gloves and chucked them into the swing-top bin. 'All over — we'll see you in six months for a check-up,' he said, standing and handing the woman out of the dental chair.

She thanked him in heavily accented English. Then she and her mother-in-law spoke to each other in Urdu, Hugh supposed it was. Her husband, using the colloquial English of the area, was already fixing up the paperwork with the receptionist.

Hugh smiled at the nurse, who was stowing instruments in the sterilizer, and undid his white jacket.

'Heading home early — Lorna's got her group tonight,' he said. 'You'll lock up, won't you, Sandra?'

'Of course. See you in the morning,' she smiled.

He smiled back and didn't disabuse her.

*

Fenny looked up at the fluorescent-lighted windows over *Roses are Red*, the flower shop, as she passed. She nearly thought of visiting her father, but she changed her mind. The venetian blinds were open, and strips of light showed in his surgery, but she thought she didn't want to sit waiting with the patients till he was through, just in order to get a lift home when it was raining. And he'd ask awkward questions about why she'd been in this part of town.

Kids at school teased her because he was a dentist. They also thought because of that he must make a lot of money, but Fenny knew that he didn't make as much as if he'd had a private practice. She wished he and her mother hadn't had political involvements at college. Other people's idealism got in the way: her father believed in health for the common man, and both her parents believed in equality of educational opportunity. Fenny was called four-eyes because of her glasses when she was little, and now she was labelled with rude names because she worked hard at school and was in the top sixth form set. It made life hard.

Patrick, the favoured, had got a prep school place, and Fenny blamed her mother for weakness and lack of conviction: how could she belong to a women's group and yet sacrifice her daughters' education and favour her son? Was it really because Patrick was a hyperactive pain in the arse who needed small classes and strict discipline? It was surely a betrayal of parental ideals, of the worst kind.

She hated her mother! She wouldn't go home and cook supper for the kids: she'd go to the library instead.

In the library, a modern building, Fenny headed first for the cloakroom. She dumped her school bag on the floor and looked at herself in the mirror. Her hair was full of rain-droplets, and because of the dampness it was fluffier than usual. She combed it down and remade the pony tail, stretching her black velvet scrunchie over it several times until it was tight enough.

Then she went into a cubicle, in order to be alone. There were graffiti on the inside of the door, 'Karen loves Lucy' and a heart. She wondered if her mother had that sort of feeling about the women at the group.

She took her prescription out of her bag, looked at the tiny, day-labelled white pills, and read the instruction leaflet carefully. She thought about the young white-coated doctor who'd examined her: weight, breasts exam, blood pressure, internal. The internal had been horrible: so had the questionnaire. Had she ever been pregnant? Of course not! She was a schoolgirl, wasn't she? Well, it was a valid question, but did she look like that sort of girl? Yes, she'd had sex: it hadn't been much fun, it hadn't really worked. She and Jeff had both been a bit sloshed, a bit giggly, a bit embarrassed at the time. The condom had proved more than a bit of a problem.

After the examination, the doctor had become more human. She'd asked if Fenny had any questions. She'd smiled across the desk, and Fenny had thought suddenly that here was a person you could talk to: not like her mother, infinitely old and bound up with her own problems, but available and offering her time.

The doctor, like Fenny, wore spectacles. They were very large, white-framed, and looked expensive. She had a wedding ring and two other rings, on different fingers, and her hair was shoulder-length and very silky, caught back on one side with a black and gold slide. She was beautiful, Fenny thought, and found herself beginning to cry.

The doctor had then pushed a box of tissues across the desk, without saying anything.

After a while, Fenny had blown her nose and apologized.

'Do you really want to go on sleeping with your boyfriend?' the doctor had asked.

'I don't know,' Fenny had said. 'Everybody does it. If I

don't, they'll think I'm dumb.'

'It's your own decision,' the doctor had said. 'You mustn't let what other people expect influence your choices. You've got your whole life ahead of you, and if you don't want sex just yet, you can say no.'

'I'm no good at saying no,' Fenny had said. 'I always say yes. Like when my mother wants me to watch my kid sister and brother, or my father wants me to become a dental hygienist, and my mother wants me to be a professional violinist because I've reached Grade Eight already — I don't seem to exist,' she said, thinking of the people in the bus.

'What do you want to do?' the doctor had asked.

'I don't know. I want to know why I don't,' Fenny had said.

She heard another woman come into the cloakroom, and decided to vacate her cubicle and go into the library to do her homework. As she washed her hands, she looked at her face in the mirror and thought about the face that looked back at her. She wondered if there were, as the doctor said, lots of girls like herself who had an overdeveloped sense of duty to other people. Usually oldest children, apparently. How interesting that was. She wanted to release them, as well as herself, from the terrible trap, if it was truly so.

As she looked for a free desk, she passed the reference books section. She found herself scanning the shelves for the medical register: when she took it down, she looked up under the Rs until she came to Ramsay. There were a number of Ramsays, and she ran her finger down the page to find what she wanted. The label pinned to the white coat had said Dr Kitty Ramsay.

Fenny read up Kitty Ramsay's career so far: her medical school, exams passed (there seemed a fair number of those) and her present work and address. Then she closed the book, and stood for a moment hugging it to her chest. Dr Fenella Carmichael? She saw the white card pinned to her lapel. Immediately she realized that she still had the problem: now she wanted to please — or even to be — Kitty Ramsay.

Then she read up, in a booklet about university applications, the requirements for medical schools: it wasn't possible to become Kitty. She wasn't taking the right subjects, because she'd been persuaded by her mother to include Music in her A-levels. And anyway, who could get those grades from the comprehensive? Even the posh-area comprehensive where the rich pinko-liberals, like her family, lived? Fenny paused, trying to think positive, and turned to the section on psychology. That was what she'd do: that would help her understand herself, and her family, and why they all quarrelled and squabbled so much. She could become a family counsellor or a social worker...she hadn't fancied the gory side of medicine, anyway.

*

Hugh had refined his plan. First he drove quickly towards home, rehearsing what he'd have to say to Lorna. Now the decision was made, he felt very calm and clear-headed. Stopped at a red light, he punched the buttons of the radio, looking for Radio Three. On the local station, there was talk of traffic jams and long tail-backs because of the rain. A cyclist had been killed in an accident. Hugh's heart jumped a beat: then he remembered Fenny hadn't ridden her bike to school this morning for some reason. His fright reminded him that he cared about Fenny: she was the only one. Poised on the edge of womanhood, she'd brush past him in the passage, wearing her owly specs and black jeans and smelling of Calvin Klein's *Obsession*.

Anyway, he felt a twinge for Fenny. He didn't want to muck up her A-levels for her. But life was hell, otherwise, dragging oneself to work every day, patching up holes in the teeth of the proletariat, had lost its appeal, and you couldn't do anything really worthwhile on the National Health any more. Lorna was obsessed with discovering her higher self and saving the otters, or whatever they were…her ideals were still intact, but she screamed at the kids and had made it clear that an early night was for reading A.S. Byatt or catching up with her committee papers for the school board.

He thought he'd found Radio Three —a piece from *Carmen* was playing, the dance which ends in her death. But when the music ended, a cheerful disc jockey's voice announced that it was the end of his show for today. Hugh thought he might have known: popular classics for easy listening…the next record was a Scott Joplin rag. He remembered that film, when he and Lorna were just married…he couldn't recall the name, but the rag was a mockery…the film was something sharp…it was *The Sting*…the sting was in the tail, he thought, parking outside his dark and empty house.

He went upstairs, pulled out a suitcase and threw clothes inside, the sort of clothes he'd have taken to a conference, followed by the conference papers themselves. On top, he chucked inside the syringe and the three ampoules he'd taken from the surgery. Designer drugs, he thought. Then he found a piece of paper and began a note to Lorna, but he'd only written 'Darling, I forgot it was today…' when he heard the front door, and his guts twisted at the voices of his children.

*

'Mum dragged me all across town for my cello lesson and then Miss Bagshaw wasn't even teaching today, she'd got the flu,' Amelia said.

'Oh poppet, I'm sorry,' Hugh said, ruffling Amelia's hair absent-mindedly.

'Don't do that, I'm feeling carsick!' Amelia snapped. 'It's sexual harassment — I'm thirteen next week!'

Stung by his daughter, Hugh moved away. There was a squealing sound in the next room, and Patrick came in carrying his hamster. Hugh saw it was Patrick squeaking, not the hamster. He hated Patrick's immaturity and wanted to strangle him: that behaviour was what prep school was supposed to knock out of him.

'Patrick! You'll scare the animal to death!' he roared.

'Patrick's mental,' Amelia said. She had fetched a glass of milk and three chocolate biscuits. She put them down on the coffee table, without a plate, threw herself on to the sofa and opened a Judy Blume paperback.

'I thought you were feeling sick — and don't you have homework?' Hugh said.

'Leave her alone.' Lorna had come into the room carrying a stoneware casserole. She turned to Hugh. 'Good. You're home early. Fenny's not back yet, and I've got to go — we're doing a vegetarian pot luck supper, husbands excluded.'

Hugh realized his younger children would be alone. He thought about staying a few hours, just till Fenny got back.

'I could sign in late to the conference,' he said. He hoped she would say yes. If she said yes, and showed she wanted him to stick around, he'd change his decision.

Lorna didn't say yes. What she said was, 'Don't hang around here on our account. I'm sure all those dentists with their gleaming white teeth are far more interesting than we are.'

*

Fenny hadn't noticed the time. She was devouring John Bowlby's description of deprivation and its effects in childhood. She thought she could really identify with this. Her mother, always a feminist, hadn't nurtured her enough, and her dissociated feelings were the result...

She felt a tap on her shoulder. One of the librarians was there. 'We're closing now. It's nine o'clock.'

'God!' Fenny said. 'I'm supposed to be minding my kid brother and sister. Mum's going to kill me!'

All the way home, she pictured Lorna's angry face and the accusation. 'Fenny? I suppose you were hanging out with Jeff again. You're so irresponsible. I missed my women's group because of you...'

How could she walk in and say that she'd just made her big career decision — she was going to study psychology and train as a family therapist?

*

At the top of the hill, Hugh got out of the car. The ground was rutted and muddy, and the wind moaned through the trees. From this spot, you could see the whole valley below. It was the spot where he'd asked Lorna…where they'd decided to marry. The valley was dark then, seventeen years ago. Today, it was dotted with little orange lights, almost like Christmas decorations. They marked the roads built during the intervening years.

A man came out of the trees with a dog bounding before him. It seemed late to be walking a dog, and Hugh didn't want to be seen by the man. He ducked back inside the car.

When man and dog had driven off in their Range rover, Hugh got out and fetched the suitcase, and the garden hose, from the boot. He fixed the hose how he wanted, then got into the car, shutting the windows and running tape along where there might be cracks. He took three ampoules out of his bag. Then he rolled up his shirt sleeve, the left arm, and looked for a vein. It wasn't easy: he was used to injecting into the gum, or the roof of the mouth, not the arm. Eventually, he managed to find a suitable place, and injected. Then he turned the key, and with the engine, the car radio came on. He recognized Tchaikovsky's First Piano Concerto: it was not his favourite piece, but it would have to do.

*

Kate was leading the women's meeting. 'Look in your partner's eyes, and describe what you see.'

Lorna held hands with Jen, her partner, across their folded knees and stared into the green depths. She could see black pupils and yellow flecks.

'Sincerity,' Jen said.

Lorna's heart flipped.

'Truth,' someone else said of their partner, 'truth and loyalty.'

'Good. and what does Lorna see?'

'Suffering,' Lorna said.

'Suffering?'

'It's in everybody's eyes — the human condition is one of suffering, and there isn't any hope, there isn't any out!' said Lorna. She dropped Jen's hands and began to cry, great painful sobs unlike anything which had happened in years. She'd remembered this morning that it was their wedding anniversary, and on such an appropriate day, she'd decided, planned, to walk out. Taking no clothes, lest anyone should suspect. She'd just disappear, change her name…they might get the police, look for her in the river, but they wouldn't find a thing… Stuff them all, she'd thought. Them and the school board and everyone else…she'd accepted the wardenship of a women's refuge, that was real life.

*

The sense of anti-climax turned into acute worry when Fenny got out of the bath. It was half-past eleven. The house was quiet. Amelia and Patrick were asleep. She realized her mother was still not home. Why? The women's group always finished at half-past nine.

She sat watching the TV, trying to drink hot cocoa instead of biting her nails. At one a.m. she remembered that TV was all-night now. She couldn't phone the police — what did one say, anyway? She didn't want to make a fuss by phoning the hospitals — her mother would be furious if she did that. Anyway, she sort-of didn't want to know if her mother had been in an accident.

Her was father on that dental conference. She looked on the kitchen pin board and found a note with the conference centre number on it. She stood beside the phone wondering whether to call him, but thought he'd be cross, too, to be woken up needlessly.

In the end, she decided her mother's group had gone on late — after all, they had been having a party, hadn't they? She got a hot-water bottle and went into her mother's room to write a note.

The note said, 'Don't bother getting up in the morning, have a lie-in for once. I'll get the kids off to school. Luv, Fenny.' She added a P.S. 'I've made a big career decision — I'm going to be what they call a family therapist. Don't try to stop me — it's very *socially meaningful.*'

Then she saw her mother's sleeping pills. Nobody should take someone else's prescribed medicine, she knew, but she'd never sleep alone in the house with only the kids. She opened the bottle, shook the pills out, and broke one in half. Half a pill shouldn't hurt, she thought, swallowing it down.

*

In the morning, she was woken by someone banging on the front door. It was a policeman. There was a police woman behind him.

'Mum?' Fenny gasped, standing on the prickly doormat in her bare feet. Her hands grasped at her open mouth, and she knew she was looking like someone in a film.

'Is your mother in?' the policeman asked.

'I don't know. I thought you knew. I thought that was

why you'd come.'

'Knew what?'

'About Mum.'

'Can we come in? It's about your father…'

It was after she'd found her mother hadn't been home all night that she noticed the date of the dental conference on the calendar. It wasn't until the next week.

Sociologists don't paint nice cosy Christmas cards

(1994/5)

For years before she married Will, her second husband, Jo had been an artist. People who came to see her shows always commented that it seemed like the work of two people: some pictures of her growing child, Rebecca, a round and naked toddler in the bath, or clad in denims and a sun hat, chewing an apple and sitting on a swing. Others the agonising twisted almost-abstracts of homeless people, beggars, old age pensioners, surrounded by their pathetic possessions in falling-down kitchens and bedrooms full of broken furniture. These were often photographs, or taken from photographs. She didn't know why she did them: she supposed, she said to the young reporter who came from the local paper, that she had some comment to make, something to say. She was powerless to do anything.

She and her first husband, Rupert, both taught art and made it. His medium was sculpture. Huge clanking metallic shapes, or wood carved into twisted, muscular pieces (for example, his *Japanese Wrestlers* or *Horse falling at a Fence*).

The fact that they both portrayed suffering and pain was not lost on the reporter: especially not later, when he wrote up Rupert's death. Rupert was found in his car – a black sporty Capri, G-reg (the old Gs, not the new ones) with mock leopard skin seat covers and a sound system which could blare country music around the inside like a mawkish social commentary inside a tin box. He'd attached a hose to the exhaust pipe, not very original, and taken a bottleful of antidepressants, just to make sure.

It choked her up. Jo couldn't believe life really meant that to Rupert: Rupert who played the clown at Becky's birthday parties, and dressed up to take her trick-or-treating at Halloween.

*

Six years later she met Will. She was teaching his son on a school holiday art project. The other children were mostly pretty ordinary. Matt was sensitive, quiet, and well mannered: he stood out. Also, his face was strangely scarred.

She was teaching them pottery: every evening, when they came to give their work in, Matt screwed his up, back into the ball of red clay he'd first started with so he'd have nothing to take home at the end. If he'd been younger she'd have made him do something nice for mum and dad, but he was twelve, too old for that kind of treatment. She let him do it, screw up the clay at the end of the session.

On the last day, his father was very late fetching him. (Evening Surgery dragged on, it turned out.) Sitting out on the steps of the community centre, waiting, she shared a bag of chips with Matt and Becky. It was a blue and gold early

September evening, the day before Matt was due to go back to boarding school.

'What's school like?' she asked him.

'It's all right.'

'Only all right?'

'It stinks, but I have to do it. Dad works all hours, you see.'

'I was at boarding school,' she said. 'It makes you devious.' She watched his face. Slowly, he smiled. His smile was crooked, caught at the right-hand corners of the mouth and eye by the scar tissue from whatever accident it had been – she hadn't asked.

'We're allowed to keep gerbils in the biology lab. I let mine breed and sell the babies. It makes enough to buy aircraft magazines with.'

Cynics might say Jo married Will to give Matt a break, but that wasn't it. Nor to give Becky a father, because she was fourteen and needed an opposite-sex parent. She had been unsure about doing it, afraid that somehow Rupert's death had been her fault, and not wanting to live the same bit of life over again. Only Will's appreciation of life, despite his profession, seemed inexhaustible. Inexhaustible so that he would drop down on the sofa after their supper together, the CD of Mozart's *Marriage of Figaro* on the player, and sleep straight through the whole opera, a smile on his lips, waking at 10 o'clock for a cup of tea and a chocolate Hobnob before going home to his huge, cold house on the other side of Wyechester. Jo used to do the ironing to the arias while he slept.

Will explained his son's strange scars. His ex-wife, Ellen, had Munchhausen's syndrome by proxy, and she had deliberately scalded her child when he was two years old.

That was why Will, among only ten percent of fathers, had custody of his son.

The first concert they went to together was the traditional Nine Lessons and Carols at Matt's school. She would always remember how the darkness in the chapel felt, like velvet hangings before her eyes. The dark space smelt of old books, musty religion and mothers' expensive perfume. Then a single treble voice pierced the gloom: Matt singing *Once in Royal David's City*. Will told her afterwards that the music master had trained up an understudy that term, in case Matt's voice broke in the last crucial weeks – he was growing so fast. But it hadn't. Her first experience of Matt in context, Matt as part of the Griffon school, was of this angel voice, the light in the darkness, beatific, unrepresentative, and desperately poignant.

A single taper lighted the choir as they stood in the porch, and then as they processed forwards, many tapers lit their way, and from these the congregation lit their own candles and tapers, until the whole chapel filled with light. She caught sight of Matt's face, the scars evident even in the candlelight. Jo had been raised without religion, and that Christmas carol meant festival to her, but not faith, not love. She and Rupert had found Becky's school nativity plays embarrassing. Now something hard inside her, something which had lain there since Rupert's death, began to melt, and she let the tears pour down her face, ruining her makeup.

Will thought it had something to do with Matthew's scars. It wasn't just the scarred face, and the angel voice. It was something without a name, something Jo could not explain. Will squeezed her hand, as they listened to the headmaster reading John's account: *the light shines in the darkness, and the darkness has not overcome it.* Then there was hope.

Jo remembered this scene, six years later, as she neared the end of a walk with Will's dog, Cleo. The poplars by the canal stretched skywards like a row of sixty-odd grey skeletons silhouetted against the angry chill of the greying sky, iron-grey, deep and icy, the bones of the poplars rattling in the wind.

Along the opposite bank, gardens stretched down to the canal. Little boats bobbed at their moorings, tiny barques for rowing gently down the stream on a summer evening, all pink clouds, sloping sunlight and children's voices. Today, though, the sticks and ragged leftover leaves of winter shrubs lurked in the long gardens as the three o'clock dusk cloaked everything in gloom.

Two cyclists and a jogger crowded past, slithering in the mud. She whistled to the dog. She tried to make it seem as if she was more than one person alone. She wanted them to know she was not afraid. She was afraid. A jogger might turn out to be that sinister thing, 'a man pretending to be a jogger, who raped three women on three separate occasions down on the beach': she'd seen that item on the news.

The dog came, bouncing on spring-like feet, her tongue lolling, saliva at the corners of her mouth. Jo threw another stick, and the dog chased after it. She turned, called the dog, clanked over the metal lifting bridge, and passed the narrowboat where steam issued from the short chimney into the frozen air. It was quite dark by the time they reached home.

So long ago, that carol service seemed: now Becky was twenty, Matt was eighteen, Will's hair was going grey, her hormones were swinging through the changes of middle age, and somewhere, she supposed, eternity was getting on with light in darkness, but it didn't seem to change the world.

When she'd moved, with Becky, into Will's large, cold, forbidding house, she had asked him to have the fir trees cut down. They stood in an ordered row at the end of the drive, pointed, deep green, and forbidding. Without them, the front windows admitted a hundred percent more light. Gradually, she'd painted the rooms, thrown out the old furniture and bought new. She'd felt very self-indulgent changing Will's house, but he was caught up in the health service reforms, devising a scheme for Wyechester GPs to band together into a non-fundholding consortium. She suggested a newsletter to keep all forty practices informed, and began to produce it on their computer at home, adding cartoon drawings to lighten the data – facts and figures about how the consortium's purchasing compared with that of fundholders, how drugs budgets were being cut by generic prescribing, and other bread and butter information about hospitals and numbers of beds.

It was one day as she leafed through a brightly coloured, glossy tabloid medical newspaper which plopped free through the letterbox every Thursday, that she discovered that at least one other GP's wife had thought of her answer to bringing more life into the house, which seemed to have grown since the children went away to college. The advert read, 'Doctor's wife offers B and B at reasonable prices. H and C in all rooms, full English breakfast, near station...'

Well, there was a big teaching hospital in Wyechester, a supply of respectable young people needing somewhere to live….

'What do the medical students do – what do the housemen do – about accommodation these days?' She asked Will, looking over the top of the practice copy of the *British Medical Journal*, which was propped against the marmalade.

'What we did – damp flat in old basements or the terraces in the east end of town,' he replied. 'Why?'

'I was thinking of the size of this house,' Jo said. 'You said Ellen had the idea of buying a big place and running a nursery school…'

'Goodness knows what destruction she could've wrought,' Will said, and he shook his head. 'If we hadn't have discovered her illness. She and I talked about having a large family as well. I've been wondering if we ought to move: just the four of us rattling about.'

'We don't rattle. Not so you'd notice. But we only use three bedrooms, and there are eight. I could advertise – we could – we could maybe do a B and B – just for the medical students or housemen, not for the public.' She thought, Will would be more accepting of a limited, defined population. She fancied cooking full English breakfast for them: she would buy an Aga – and the cat would lie in front of it while the bacon sizzled and the croissants (well never mind they weren't English) heated in the cool oven.

*

By the next Christmas Eve Jo and Will had a house full of

medics, all 'on take' over the holiday. That afternoon at two o'clock the travellers rolled up the drive in their van. Jo took very little notice. She just glanced from the window, round the Christmas tree, to see if they were still there, when she pulled the curtains at four against the deep thick darkness of mid-December. They were. A little snow was falling, and the man was feeding the dog outside the van. An oil lamp burnt at its window.

Will came home at seven-fifteen. 'Sorry – we've had a busy day,' he said, hanging up his coat. 'They've all got post-flu coughs and depression. There's nothing I can do – time is the only healer, the doctor isn't God these days.'

'Maybe it was better when people didn't have such high expectations of the health service,' Jo said. 'Maybe it was better when there was no health service – they didn't expect so much.'

'The bad old days may be coming back – private GPs could be the thin end of the wedge of a two-tier system worse than fundholding has brought in.' Will said. 'Anyway, what's the van doing in the drive?'

'Travellers. I let them park there, they've nowhere else to go. I passed three beggars coming home from the shops: you don't know what to do.'

'They're the sort of people the Care in the Community Act has put on the streets,' Will said. He sighed, and began taking glasses from the sideboard, and pouring himself a whisky. 'Do you want one of these?' He asked her.

'Maybe we should ask them to join us for dinner?' she replied, shaking her head about the drink.

'Are you serious?'

She looked at him. He was obviously tired, and had had

enough of suffering humanity. 'No,' she said.

Will was rotaed on for Christmas day, so they planned to eat their Christmas dinner on the evening of Christmas Eve. The turkey was in the Aga, the pudding steaming in a pot, and Becky laying the table with red candles, holly and ivy twined around their holders, and crackers at every place, when the doorbell rang. Becky opened the door.

Jo looked out past Becky at the shabby vehicle parked in the drive. It had once been an ambulance, but now ragged curtains hung at the windows, bells and amulets jingled at the windscreen. The couple on the step, the man with dreadlocks and a dog on a rope, the pregnant girl wearing a long Indian dress and a leather jacket, stared back. 'We heard you do bed and breakfast,' the girl said.

'Mum puts up some of the trainee doctors from the hospital,' Becky said. She leaned on the doorframe, herself a respectable version of the other girl. She was a second-year art student, studying fashion design, and her clothes were as off the wall as the girl's, merely a little tidier and a good deal cleaner. Both Becky and the traveller girl had rings on every finger, dancing earrings, and a musky perfume of incense.

Nonetheless, Jo moved Becky aside. 'We don't have any rooms to let,' she said, quite honestly, but thinking of Will's need for peace and quiet this evening. 'They're all taken.' She heard him come up behind her. He looked over her shoulder, saying nothing.

'Her baby's due,' the man said calmly, like a statement. The dog sniffed Jo's shoe. The girl's pregnant stomach seemed to thrust forward, emphasising her partner's point. 'What are we going to do? It's freezing in the van.'

'Find somewhere else,' Jo said, and she shrugged.

'That's right – it looks as if you need somewhere, but we're full up with trainee doctors from the hospital,' Will said.

'Don't they go home for Christmas?' the man asked.

'Who would run the place then?' Will asked. 'Illness doesn't keep Christmas as a holiday.'

'Oh, Mum,' Becky said. 'Dad?'

'Don't oh Mum – where would they sleep? Your room?' Jo asked.

'They could stay in the drive, and at least have a bit of Christmas dinner.'

'We'll bring some out to you,' said Jo. She felt uncomfortable, looked at Will and Becky, thought about stretching the food to feed two more mouths.

A little later, carving the turkey, Will said, 'What I don't want is for that girl to go into labour. I'm not delivering her baby there – you do understand that? They can stay the night in the drive but in the morning they go.'

'That is not my stepfather talking,' Becky said.

'Oh yes it is,' Will said, and he waggled the carving knife at her. 'Litigation is what you would get, delivering a baby in a van like that with no proper equipment. She goes to hospital, if she has as much as a pang. She isn't my patient – I've no idea what her pregnancy's been like. Quite possibly she's had no antenatal care at all.'

*

It was dark, icy cold, and still. Jo knew why she had come awake like this: Will had gone out to a patient, and the slight movement of him leaving the bed, the soft closing of the front door, had brought her into consciousness. She lay for a moment, and then she remembered it was Christmas Eve, and that he was not on call until tomorrow morning. Earlier, they had agreed that they'd place Matt and Becky's surprise stockings in their rooms in the early morning – it was hopeless trying to wait up until they came in from celebrating with their friends, but they'd probably sleep, after that, until noon. So the stockings, a pair of Will's skiing socks, lay on the dressing table, like pregnant snakes full of intriguing bulges. Playing Father Christmas was not what Will had gone to do.

She got out of bed, and went to the window to see if the car had gone. It hadn't. It crouched outside, a black BMW scattered with a thin covering of snow. Snow was falling, silently, on the drive and on the travellers' van. The dog sat in the snow outside the van, and the oil lamp burnt at the window. The double doors at the back were partly open. A man was kneeling there: not the man with the dreadlocks, but Will.

That girl was in labour, she thought immediately. They'd come and got him out of bed. She pulled on warm trousers under her nightdress, thrust her feet into her boots, and went downstairs. Her coat was on the hook by the door, their own dog lay on the mat, and the door was on the latch, admitting freezing air. Jo, bundled into her coat, crossed the garden, and the travellers' dog whimpered at her. She put out her hand for it to sniff, 'Good dog, good dog,' she said softly. It shuffled its legs in the snow: it was tethered to the van. From inside, she heard the girl's cries, and the man, 'One more push, Carol – the head's crowning, you heard the doctor say.'

She watched Will's back as he leaned over the girl, who

was lying on a sleeping bag covered with what looked like two of their best bath towels. After the girl's last cry, as the body of the child shot out, there was silence. Jo tensed. Now the baby should cry. Instantly, she thought she knew. It was dead. What would they say to Will, she thought. If it were a dead baby, who was responsible, who would take the blame?

As Will had said, they weren't his patients. She'd probably had no antenatal care. Delivering a baby like this was like helping at the scene of an accident: you could be liable, you didn't want to get involved. She felt the sweat pour down inside her nightdress, and realised she felt more anxiety for Will and his career than compassion for the parents. The snow fell fast: penitential snow, a silent witness to death at Christmas.

Then suddenly, she heard the baby cry. At the same time a chorus began overhead. She realised her tears were flowing, the way they had in the chapel at the Griffon school, when Matt sang his solo. That was the song – *Gloria in Excelsis* – a carol from the service six years ago. The snow was illuminated, as if all the house lights were on. Becky must have got up and put them on. Now Will was stepping backwards out of the van. He turned and saw her, without surprise. 'Jo, ring for an ambulance, would you?'

'But the baby's all right!' She said.

'We're almost out of the wood – but we're waiting for the placenta to be born – so do it for me, can you? They like to take unintentional home deliveries in for a check-up.' There was blood smeared on his shirt, and on his gloved hands.

'I thought it was dead,' she said. 'Why didn't it cry?'

'I thought so too. The cord was round his neck. I don't know how I sorted that one out, and without resuscitation equipment, but I did.'

'Some kind of a miracle,' Jo said.

'Experience,' Will said, and he climbed back into the van.

Jo went into the house, to use the phone. The chorus continued outside. Inside it was dark. No one had put the house lights on. The lights were outside, over the travellers' van.

The Way the Cookie Crumbles

(SEPTEMBER 1993)

Megan Simms, in her purple cardigan and her grey skirt, sits in front and a little to the side of Alex Henderson. Megan squeezes a grey-white hanky in her hand: it is balled-up and damp, not from crying but from her nervous, sweaty hand. Megan learned a long while ago not to cry, and she has not cried for months. Not since Mother's funeral.

Alex, perplexed, searches his mind for a solution to Megan's appearances regularly on Monday morning in his surgery. He is in a kind of caring despair. Tranquillisers and antidepressants haven't shifted Megan's misery and her pale, fish-like eyes scrutinise his face once more this morning. He clears his throat: he has the beginnings of a summer cold.

'Have you thought of counselling?' he asks.

'I can't afford private treatment,' Megan says. She explains how her job as part-time receptionist to a chiropodist doesn't pay well, and that she can't seem to sell the house where she and Mother lived — the house where she grew up.

If she ever has grown up. If she hasn't just grown older, sliding imperceptibly from a dull, lack-lustre and lonely child standing on the edge of the playful, shouting group to a dim, short-sighted, unathletic teenager in a grey pleated skirt who had trouble with her period pains and quite appalling acne. And so to a middle-aged young woman in clothes better suited to an elderly person living in an old-age home.

Malcolm McKay, the senior partner, had watched the transformation of Megan from late-teenager to middle-aged woman, and then, almost cleverly, succumbed to a stroke just around the time Mother died, leaving Alex Henderson to pick up and reassemble the scattered pieces. Megan had found Malcolm a wonderful father-figure: Alex knew that unfortunately she thought him wonderful too.

When Mother finally died, Megan threw her arms around him in the dim, urine-scented, fusty bedroom and declared that he, Dr Henderson, was now the only person she had in the world. While Mother lay prudently dead upon the bed, her eyes tactfully closed. Alex, disentangling himself, handed her the tissue-box and wrote out a prescription for sleeping tablets to tide her over the first few agonizing days of mourning.

'How about if it's on the National Health?' Alex asks now. 'You wouldn't have to pay...'

Megan brightens. Wanly, she smiles, and passes the balled-up hanky from hand to hand. 'I'll try anything you suggest, Dr Henderson,' she says bravely.

They discuss the counselling centre. Megan says that it's only down the road from the chiropodist's practice, and she could go in her lunch hour. Alex smiles and says isn't that good?

*

The woman counsellor has a green tweedy skirt and a green jumper in a rather harsh kind of bright green: she doesn't smile like Alex or Dr McKay. She leads Megan down a passage to the big bright room where there are enough chairs for a small tea party to assemble. This is because the Centre holds Group Therapy sessions on other days.

The woman signals Megan to sit on one of the armless, tweedy chairs to one side. Not just any of the chairs, but one which is placed, tastefully, no doubt, half-behind a wicker screen, at a right-angle to another chair which the counsellor settles upon. Between the two chairs is a small square table and on the table there is nothing but a box of tissues.

For when the clients cry.

You see, everything has been thought of.

On the wall, an efficient electric clock marks out the time for the fifty-minute hour.

The woman asks Megan why she has come. When she says because Dr Henderson referred her, the woman looks blank. Megan explains who Alex is, and the woman shakes her head. She has not heard of him: she comes into town from a village somewhere, retaining her anonymity.

Megan looks at the box of tissues: you can take those away, for a start, she wants to say. But before the counsellor, she becomes dumbly obedient, fitting her remarks to replies in a steady, colourless voice.

They talk about Mother's death: the woman asks questions in the same dull, lacklustre voice. Sometimes she repeats back Megan's own words to her, like a kind of brass mirror held up, showing her what a poor, inadequate creature Megan is.

Megan already knows this.

It is to heal the inadequacy that she has come here.

The woman's hands lie on her lap in an open position, like the curved wrapping paper just taken off a parcel. It could be the parcel of Megan's life, the burden of elderly, wearing-out, dying parents she's had to bear. Or it could be the parcel she never unwrapped: the parcel of her virginity.

'I never got further education: you see, I was needed at home. I took the first year of an English degree and then Father had his stroke: Mother couldn't manage alone, I was needed at home.'

'But that was twenty years ago!' the woman says.

To Megan, it is like yesterday. It took the two of them, she and Mother, to turn him in the bed.

'Father was incontinent after that,' Megan adds helpfully in a small voice that conceals her bitterness. Wet, stinking sheets are no joke when you don't know a strong, healthy man of your own to counteract the disgust at the drooping male organ, the flabby, wasted flesh.

Hands still in their open position, the woman asks Megan to tell her some more about herself. Megan knows nothing about the woman: Dr McKay had a wife and a son, Robbie, and grandchildren: this nameless woman is a blank sheet. She betrays nothing. Megan, glancing at the hands, notes there are no rings: spinster or divorced?

'Most people have a career, if they don't have a family,' Megan says, and she thinks of the woman's lack of rings. 'I am the chiropodist's part-time receptionist: it is not a career.'

'Aren't you glad you've got a job to do?' the woman asks.

'No,' Megan thinks. The chiropodist is quite obviously gay, and regards himself as some kind of foot-artist. Megan has worked for him ever since Father's death.

Another low-voiced question breaks into the utter stillness of the room. 'How do you feel about your work?'

Megan wants to say the word: Bloody. She has never said it. Bloody fucking hell, she could say, I hate being. Would the woman react? She thinks not. The woman is a cold fish, in Megan's opinion.

She thinks about her work: answer phone, tick off appointment, sweep floor. Especially sweep floor. Floor is scattered, after one of Mr Ormerod's sessions, with flakes of human skin, the things of which corns are made.

The woman waits.

Megan says, 'I came to learn a bit about how to function now that Mother's gone.'

The woman says, 'Tell me about Mother.'

She would rather the woman told her a few scraps about herself. Does she have a cat, a garden, friends? A bit of to and fro wouldn't come amiss in this non-conversation. The woman holds the brass mirror, and in it Megan sees the reflection of herself, moaning about Mother's demands. The hot water bottle, the pills, the library book (detective or costume drama, nothing too upsetting. Megan herself re-reads the classics: George Eliot, Jane Austen, the Brontës). Help onto the commode in the morning and empty out the dark brown strong-smelling piss, sponge the pink and white body, drape it with woolly clothes – two pairs of knickers, two vests, in winter, and over those a petticoat, jersey, skirt, and cardigan.

Megan's nose is sensitive to smells: she hates the smell of Mother's room: baby powder and sweat and unwashed body. Her own body has never been seen by anyone but mother. Mother washing her in the bath, 'a lace suit all over, dear, and in between leggies – stretch them out!'

Intimacy.

'Tell me about your relationship with your brother.'

'He was killed in a motorbike accident, 1962.' There isn't more to say. His clothes hang in the wardrobe like some kind of grey cloth man, smelling of cigarettes long gone.

'What do you want to work on?'

Not, 'what do you want to work on, Megan?' She had noticed that the woman never introduced herself nor asked her client's name.

'My anger with my family.'

'They make you angry?' The woman says, holding up the brass mirror. Megan hears the words and is ashamed.

It is wrong to be angry with the family.

They can't help their messy little unproductive lives.

She sees her family pathology is her pathology, and she knows what the demands are.

'You can have five weeks: tell the receptionist when you go out you are to have five weeks.'

And that's all? Megan looks at the clock. She only got forty of the fifty-minute hour. She hesitates to assert herself and demand the other ten. Instead she rises and pulls on her navy plastic mac. The woman remains seated.

It is as if she were going to remain there forever: or at least until next week, seated in the same position, the same place, beside the box of tissues, waiting for someone to cry. Maybe she'll cry. Maybe that would break the silence.

Of course, she won't. She'll get up and go about her life. This serenity and silence is all a con, an act.

Meanwhile, Megan needs to sell the house. The yellowy-grey brick townhouse where the scenes of her life have been acted out. She goes once again to the Estate Agent, where a boy of about twenty, who has a hairstyle like a brush, tells her that if she gets the kitchen fitted up the house will be easier to sell.

*

Home again, she goes down the steps and into the coal cellar. The coal cellar smells of damp and on the walls a kind of mushroom grows, a blue-white mushroom like dead flesh. There isn't coal kept there any more, but small flakes and crumbs of leftover coal, and basketfuls of coal dust, cover the floor.

Megan looks at the beams: a beam runs the length of the cellar: she thinks about the strength of the beam, carrying the ground floor of the house, she believes.

In a corner there is a length of rope that used to be a washing line, and a broken chair: a kitchen chair. The back is loose but the seat and four legs are fine. High up on the wall there is a grating. She climbs on the chair and looks out through the grating and into the road. All she can see is the wheels of a car parked in front of the house. In what Mother had called the old days, a horse and cart had called with the coal, and the coalman, black as soot, had emptied the bags down, straight down the hole in the front path and into the cellar. From where the housemaid had carried up hods of fuel for the fires.

She goes up to the bathroom and opens the cupboard. Inside are all Father's shaving things: the things she used to shave him while he lay in bed inert as a corpse and incontinent as a baby. She takes them out.

71

She goes back to the basement, and she takes off her cardigan. Then she unfastens her skirt. It drops to the floor. She pulls her jumper, then her petticoat, over her head. She removes her vest, tights, knickers, and bra. They all came from Marks and Spencers. She tidies the clothes into a folded heap.

Nobody has ever seen her like this, naked and mature, white and smooth, hairy in the right places.

Megan takes the rope lying in the corner and makes a running loop, a noose. She puts it over her head. She takes Father's razor, and she slashes at her wrists.

She isn't very good at it, and the blood doesn't flow as much as she would like. She sees this as typical of herself: she isn't very good at anything, except helping old shuffling bodies on and off commodes, and spooning in custard.

She slashes other parts of her body: her thighs, her belly, her breasts. Finally she climbs onto the broken chair, attaches the rope to the beam, and kicks the chair away.

It is very cold and damp in the coal cellar. The mushrooms are blue-white, like dead flesh.

*

Alex Henderson is perplexed: he has been called out by the police to identify a body in the morgue.

The pathologist pulls the sheet back, and there's the face of Megan Simms, white and dead. The pathologist tells Alex how she was found, and that it looks as if she had been dead three days.

'Man from the estate agents with a client,' he says. 'Called the police: they had to break the door down. Bottles of milk and letters in the box, obvious something was amiss.'

The pathologist shows Alex the whole body. As doctors, they survey the damage. Alex passes a hand over his face: he is confused. In his mind, he sees the body of his wife Carrie, as he comes up the stairs to bed. He is on call. She is pulling on her nightdress and he gets a glimpse of her long, straight, white back, the curve of her hips, the softness of her thighs. Then she hears him and turns, dropping the garment so it covers her from neck to toe. She is laughing. He sees Carrie to block out Megan for an instant. Then he shakes his head, and the pathologist replaces the sheet.

'There was a note: to Dr Henderson. It's why we called you to identify, in the absence of relatives.' The pathologist hands Alex the note.

'I have seen myself in the mirror: it was not very nice.' In Megan's neat handwriting.

Alex goes to the surgery. He works through his list of evening patients. Periodically, as he palpates an abdomen or listens to a chest, he sees Megan's lacerated body in his mind, and shakes his head to clear away the image. As he listens to the distressed, he hears her voice answering, 'I have seen myself in the mirror…'

Finally, it is seven o'clock. He drives home and lets himself into the house and there is the smell of a stew. Carrie is in the kitchen. He kisses her on the mouth, a kiss of possession and relief. He is very tired.

She says she is sorry, but supper is not ready. Alex wants to sink into a chair and do nothing. His two-year-old son, a contraceptive error they've accepted with love and a certain amount of adaptation, comes and clasps his legs, biting his knees and shrieking 'Daddy! Daddy!' The little hands are like spiders, tickling the back of his knees and the little white teeth sink into the shallow flesh. On the hall table is a letter from his stepdaughter who has gone away to college. She's reading psychology and writes about running rats through cages and observing people behaving in pubs.

'Can you bear to put the infant in the bath?' Carrie asks. 'I'm running late, he slept half the afternoon.' He knows this means she was painting in her studio and didn't notice the time.

Alex puts down his bag and lifts his son. Joshua pulls his father's right ear and laughs into it. Alex feels the weight of the child against his own exhaustion, sadness, and confusion. Why did Megan kill herself, and why the mutilation? Or if she didn't do it, who did?

In the bathroom, he peels off Joshua's clothes. The overalls are smeared with chocolate, on the bib, and mud, on the knees. The T-shirt is damp at the neck where it's been chewed. The nappy isn't wet and Joshua is keen on the idea of sitting on the pot, delighted to produce a pee. Then Josh seizes Carrie's bottle of foam bath and squeezes far too much into the bath while Alex is flushing the loo. In the bath, he splashes water so that it sprays over his father's shirt.

Alex removes his tie, which had trailed in the water like a thirsty snake. Joshua wumps a duck and a boat into the foam, and pulls all the flannels off the bath rack to join them. Alex soaps his son's back, front, and limbs, and he sees the deep red slashes on Megan's body, weeping congealed blood. He is confused.

'Daddy?' Joshua demands. 'Sing!'

Alex realises that he has been silently kneeling beside the bath, considering the whys of Megan's action.

'What does Mummy sing you in the bath?' he asks.

'Piggies!' Joshua exclaims, and he sticks a foot in the air. 'Piggies and toes!'

Zodiac

(JUNE 1989)

As I stood up to leave the bus, I realised.

I have this habit — on journeys I dream. I'd been thinking about my visit, though the arrival of a man in the strange hat, who sat himself down, firmly, two rows ahead, interrupted me. And I'd slipped it off my finger into my pocket, — the zodiac ring which André had given me all those years ago.

Now it was gone! Had it fallen out of my pocket as I stood? My eyes scanned the floor of the bus. Or had it fallen earlier, as I gazed out of the window at the passing countryside, musing on today's events?

Strange, unreal, to spend time with André again after twenty years. I'd taken the long-distance bus, instead of the car, and arrived at his studio just as I had when we were students, wearing blue jeans (designer, now, not the old patched Levis) and a sweatshirt with *Bliss* emblazoned across the front. Very bold to buy that, I'd thought, as the assistant carefully folded the shocking pink garment around some tissue paper, popped it into a bag, and rang up my purchase. André would love it, I pictured his face, enlivened by a broad smile.

From the coach station I'd walked, my feelings a mix of excitement and apprehension, looking for the address he'd given in his letter. Noticing the numbers, it would be some way down. The road was narrow, grey, depressing. So many paving stones were cracked, or splodged with chewing gum or other, nameless, sticky stains. I passed a newsagent's, a chemist, an Asian grocery store, a coin-operated laundry with a health and fitness workshop above. At last, here was the number: a blue painted door, paint peeling around that number, a bell on the side. I looked up: that must be André's studio, with windows looking down into the street. As I rang the bell I smelt spicy cooking: unlikely that was André making lunch! So, he now lived above an Indian restaurant. How was he actually doing these days? What had twenty-odd years done to him, what had he achieved, why his invitation?

Uneven, hurrying footsteps sounded from inside, and with a rattling of keys, the door was flung open, 'André!'

'Janey! Still the same!' Broad grin. Scar down his face.

'Worn by time and broader in the beam!'

'Hey, don't say a word,' arm around my waist, drawing me into the dark hallway, 'it suits you.'

We laughed. Then, feeling awkward, I looked at him properly. Unbelievable André from my student days. Not terribly changed, except for that long scar down one cheek, a bit more weight, some lines around the eyes. Otherwise, those deep brown eyes, the black hair greying but still thick and flopping forward the way it had when I'd watched him working at the easel across the room from me. He'd be shaking the hair out of his eyes, pausing and pushing it back, run his hands through...

'Janey,' he embraced me, as a long-lost friend…

'Still the same you,' I echoed, 'both elbows in holes, paint on your jeans.' I couldn't not smile with pleasure. But should I be reassured, or not, by the familiarity of the outfit? 'Can't believe it, we meet again! Somebody told me you were dead.'

'Not me. Old flames never die.'

'So of course, when I read about your private view I did a double take and wrote you that absurd letter via the gallery.'

'Didn't I hear you'd withdrawn from the world? Always a serious, Catholic girl?'

'Moi? I married the boy next-door.'

'Right…'

Going down the hall, and climbing the steep dark staircase, I noticed how much André was limping. But then, we emerged into the studio, into the sunshine. It was like popping out of a rabbit hole – a huge room filled with light, the grey weather gone. Canvasses stacked against the walls, sketches pinned or stuck to edges of shelves with masking tape, and on the table jars of brushes and pencils, and twisted tubes of paint. A large canvas was on the easel: the rough beginnings of something non-figurative. There was a kitchen corner, with a gas stove, sink and cupboards. Separated from the main studio simply by a divan bed and a couple of boards on old display stands. This was not a place where a successful creative hung out, more like a student squat.

André had an old Beatles number playing: one of their later albums. John Lennon's easily recognisable nasal voice, was chanting *I am the walrus*. Psychedelic, and strangely perfect.

'Oh – *you!*' I said, trying to sort out the present from

the deja vu.

'Of course… now listen, I thought we'd have a pub lunch.'

'Mmm, nice. Your local?'

'A better place, by the river.' What sort of a river was this?

'Just down the road, over the canal. You don't believe me? There are fields and a water-meadow.'

Yeah, I thought, André's imaginary world… 'No, listen, Janey. Living here might look to you very inner city, but down the road, over the bridge, walk a couple of hundred yards.'

We'd see. I'd already noticed a walking stick over by the door, and true to André's nature, a fancy one. Beautiful wood, and a dog's head carved on the ivory handle.

André pulled the old jumper over his head, tousling his hair, and shrugged on a faded denim jacket. 'Ready?' He took up the fancy stick with the dog's head handle.

'You okay walking? I mean, I don't need to..'

'I often do it. The walk.' So, with anyone special? I wouldn't ask.

The canal was indeed horrible: on the bank, some things had been pulled out, perhaps by the council trying to tidy up. An old pram, draped with duckweed, and a striped mattress were now disintegrating on the bank. Across on the other side was gloomy, thirties-style building, obviously a factory. 'André – tell me this isn't this is one of your fantasies.'

'Aha – but when we cross the hump-back bridge, that's one of the reasons I chose to live here, the surprises on my doorstep. Almost my doorstep.'

Sure enough, a huge surprise: coming to the top of the bridge, a stunning view! Green fields, flat and verdant – a green expanse of water-meadows stretching away towards a distant tree-lined river, shimmering through the countryside like a huge snake. Through a five-bar gate at the end of the bridge we came to a cinder path, and as we crossed the fields, towards a second bridge, a herd of cows watched lazily. Finally, we arrived at a thatched, stone-built inn, set back from the water, surrounded by hawthorn trees heavy with blossom, and picnic tables arranged beneath.

Later, a family of swans with five cygnets glided gracefully by as we ate our ploughman's lunch. 'Pretty good surprise, wouldn't you think?' André remarked.

'Yep, magical.' Our eyes met over our beer glasses, as we toasted each other in our old ironic style. Or was this ironic? 'You know, I can't believe it's happening.'

'Only believe,' André responded.

'I really did believe – that you were dead. The accident in – Turkey, wasn't it? On the road to India in that awful psychedelic-painted van, someone told me.'

He looked down into his drink, swilled it around in the glass. 'Bush telegraph got that wrong. Healing took a long time. You've noticed the leg, and the scars. But no, not dead, as you also see,' he said, touching the dog's head on his stick.

'And so you quit the drugs?'

'It made sense. But once an addict...'

'Do you go to one of those groups, like AA?'

'Something like. Janey – let's not just talk about the past. I've got something here...'

André said, reaching in the pocket of his jacket, and laid it on the table.

'The zodiac ring!'

'The ring you gave back to me.'

'You've kept it, all this time?'

A strange feeling crept over me: hope, desperation, then

an ambivalent excitement rose, and died back down, as I picked it up and turned it over, looking at the inside, then the outside. The inside silver, the outside black, with all the Zodiac in silver. I remembered how I'd said to him, 'I'm always glad Cancer isn't my sign. Like a stigma, or a fate.'

Back then he'd replied, 'What about Virgo?'

And I'd heard it as a challenge, or an invitation. We'd been very young.

I passed the ring back. 'Aren't you going to put it on?'

Now, I hesitated. Then chanced it, and held out my hand, fingers extended.

'Oh, why not?'

André held onto the ring, and my hand.

'I think, the way we did this before.'

Again, the invitation. There were reasons why not, vows, but my skin prickled with desire. A picture flashed in my head, David, Susan, Robert, my family. With an effort, I held it there, behind my eyes. David. Steady, dependable, a smart lawyer, a good provider. Janey, you are a wife, a mother.

For a moment, André held up the ring, looking through it, reminding me of another ring, a ring of power and destruction. Then he moved to replace it in the pocket of his jeans, and I felt loss like falling down a deep, dark mineshaft.

'No… oh… oh yes,' I breathed, shutting out that momentary vision of Sauron's ring. 'The way we did before.'

Hand in hand, we retraced our steps, over the bridge, across the fields, past the cows, through the five-bar gate, over the second bridge to the studio in the urban grime. I sat on the divan. André started hunting through a shelf stacked with albums, searching for music.

'Got it!' he said, pulling one out, and waving it at me. 'Soundtrack from an old musical? Yes?'

Breathless, I nodded, 'Hey, what a cover reveal. *Hair?*'

'The most controversial musical in London, 1968. Now,' he said, as the music began, 'let's go back in time – it's the Age of Aquarius.'

We took hands and embraced properly, then looked carefully each other's eyes. We are about the same height, but I noticed André had put on weight, and how his eyes were clear of the old redness. Slowly I removed his jacket, undid his shirt.

'Bliss,' he said a few moments later, as we lay together on the divan, his head against the word across my sweatshirt.

We made love unhurriedly, luxuriously, the afternoon sun illuminating the studio, the scent of paint, and turps, and bare wood, the same as I remembered from years ago, living with André, poor as church mice. Afterwards, he took the ring again, and slipped it on the middle finger of my left hand, where it had fitted perfectly the first time. Where now it was possibly a little tight, a bit constricting.

'I still want you, Janey.'

'André, you can't – it's years and years.' I laughed, dismissing it. Though secretly, I wished life had worked out differently...

'Let me draw you, okay? Before you go...' He pulled on his jeans, leaving his shirt on the floor, and changed the record. With Dylan on the player, the sun sloping from the window across the floor, a thousand shimmering motes swirling in the sunbeam. The familiar smells of the studio sharpening in the warmth.

The proverbial nun and gypsy fought within as they

always had. I thought again of David.

'Clothed, please?'

'No – I always loved your body.'

'It's too old. The years have left me with scars too.' The lump had been benign, the scar was small.

'You thought of the ring, but that isn't your sign,' André said. He touched my breast, bent and kissed the scar.

'I was glad I wasn't Cancer, yes, of course.'

'So let me draw you,' he said again.

I looked to my watch for support, 'No – I have to go.'

'Just phone – you said David was away, and those teens – they'll be glad to have the house to themselves.'

'Look – I do care about my family you know.'

'Tell me you didn't enjoy today.'

'I can't, I did. You'd better have the ring back.'

'No. You keep it. It was always yours.'

'I don't like to.'

Suddenly angry, André snarled, 'Have it. I don't want it any more.'

And I saw the whole visit had been a mistake. Hurriedly, ashamed, I dressed and fled.

At the bus station, I stood in the queue behind a man in a curious hat, a long garment. I pictured him as the Carpenter in Lewis Carroll's poem. The Walrus and the Carpenter, the old Beatles number, *I am the walrus. The Walrus and the Carpenter were walking hand in hand...*

The man sat two rows ahead: he wasn't looking round, but that hat he wore seemed to regard me throughout the journey.

I pictured David and the kids. David busy with a case in Manchester, wouldn't be there in the car to meet me from

the bus, or to kiss me as I walked in through the door. So
he wouldn't nose out betrayal, smell André on my clothes
and skin. David the perfect husband: how could I have
betrayed him?

And Susan and Robert? Who treat the house as a hotel?
Who play *Bros* and *Simply Red* top volume in their rooms?
Now it's Susan, not me, who washes her hair several times
a week. The long black skirts, gypsy earrings, denim jacket,
eccentric make-up, hers not mine.

On my way out of the bus, my eyes cast downwards,
I searched for the ring among the sweet-wrappers, crisp-
packets and old tickets. It was the terminus: I thought
everyone else had left.

'Have you lost something – was it this?' That voice
beside me: David. The back of my neck pricked, as a hand
appeared, holding out what I was looking for.

I blushed with guilt. 'Yes.'

'A strange item for you to have,' he said drily, handing
it over. This accent wasn't David's, it had a lilt of the West
of Ireland. But a real black and silver zodiac ring had been
placed in my hand.

I murmured 'Thank you,' though my voice was
hardly audible.

The priest shook his head, 'Superstitions, the opium
of the people.' His biretta still recalled the carpenter's hat.

'A gift from an artist. Of purely sentimental interest.'

All this was certainly strange. Some of the story woven
round it was true. And even nuns can dream, I thought,
looking down at the navy skirt and the silver cross of
our order. I walked slowly from the coach station to the
community house, wondering what to do with the ring.

Later, coming to pray in our chapel, I took a candle from the box beneath the statue of Our Lady, with her halo of stars, and lit it in remembrance of André. I knelt, and prayed for his soul. Somewhere in the dusty Turkish soil lay his body, the gypsy beside him. I thought of David my lawyer friend, whom I sometimes saw about the town. Neither of us had married, each other or another: our unborn children and the untried years lay between us, because of the nun, the gypsy, and André. Between André and the Church, David never stood a chance.

Whispers

(2003)

The year she gave birth to her fourth baby, Richard had unexpectedly walked back into her life. Down the hospital ward on a sleepy heatwave afternoon. He was wearing a linen jacket and carrying a present for the baby, and a jar of English Lavender bath seeds.

The other mothers mistook him for her husband.

Today, fifteen years later, the autumn light faded grey to navy as they scrunched purposefully along the shoreline, their boots denting the wet sand, their hair blown back from their faces by the threadbare touch of a chilly breeze. Anna stopped, fished a hanky from her pocket and blew her nose. All around her the salty, fishy smell of seaweed rose from the beach. She bent and picked up a long strand, running to catch up Richard.

'Seaweed,' she said, pressing it into his gloved hand.

'Bladder wrack,' he laughed, and flung it around her neck, holding her to him at arm's length. Their eyes held a moment, then 'Tea?' he asked.

'With buns?' she smiled. She wanted him to take her hand and tuck it into his pocket, to warm it. Instead he flung his arms wide and crossed them, fast, several times, to warm himself.

Words hung between them like the little coloured bulbs strung between the lamp-posts on the promenade. Climbing the pebbled beach, each step forward involved a slide back as the stones moved. Harsh neon flickered from the amusement arcade. The lighthouse on the headland beamed its light once, twice, into the twilight.

The Tea Shop modelled vintage with elegance, its interior smelling sweetly of cupcakes. Lamps on the gingham-clothed tables lit and warmed the air. They ordered Earl Grey and toasted buns.

'What a time-warp,' he smiled.

There were other customers: elderly ladies, two nuns with a priest, two women with three ice-cream-eating children.

They slid off their coats: here for a conference, without casual clothes, Richard had on, under his waxed jacket, a lounge suit, with a Liberty tie. Anna imagined the paisleys on the tie as tadpoles—then, before she stopped herself, they morphed.

Pouring tea, suppressing the symbolism, 'I wish I'd left,' she said, 'First I had the children, then I didn't have the oomph. There's nothing here but fishing and education. They both stink.' Richard smiled, eyes mischievous as ever. 'You know why I stayed,' she added.

'Because Henry was made headmaster.' Richard said.

Anna put down her cup. 'I knew, you knew, you'd be back every summer. It wasn't that Jenny and Henry would suffer as people. Wasn't there something wrong with all of us?'

In the silence, the priest and the two nuns rose, paid, and glided from the shop like muted penguins. Richard's long, bony fingers played with the pepper mill. The waitress slipped the bill under the edge of the teapot. Richard inclined his head to read the amount.

'Wasn't there?' Anna repeated. She wanted Richard on the point of a pin.

'Maybe…there was,' he said.

'And now you've got yourself out of it, you try not to think about what I have done to myself.'

'We all have our own responsibilities, to ourselves,' Richard said. 'And to our partners.'

'Waiting for your visits made my boring life with the headmaster of a minor public school almost possible. You made the wind and the sea beautiful, you told me I was valuable. I suppose I must've done something for you? Though you chose to live behind some closed door.'

'Anna.' Richard laid his hand over hers, grasping her fingers lightly.

The waitress crossed the shop, 'I'm afraid you'll have to leave now, we're closed,' she said. And turned the sign to say 'Open' to the room.

ACKNOWLEDGEMENTS:

Although she won't see the book, I'd like to dedicate this collection to my friend and encourager Liz Williams, in thanks for the fun we had over the years when we took time off to be 'ladies who lunch' and alongside the retail therapy chatted and supported one another in our work and family lives. Liz, thank you for believing in my creative work, for your generosity (to me and many others), your help with the details of medical lives, and your ever-ready smile!

Thanks also to those who helped by doing proof reading and copy-editing (you know who you are) and to Rachel Lawston for cheerfulness and the hard work of getting bare bones of a book ready for production once again.